THE POLICE KNOW EVERYTHING

Best wishes!
Sanford Phippen

THE POLICE KNOW EVERYTHING

Downeast Stories

by

Sanford Phippen

Introduction by Edward M. Holmes

Puckerbrush Press, Orono, Maine

ACKNOWLEDGEMENTS

"The Police Know Everything," "The Problems of Historical Research," and "The Lobster Stomp" have appeared in *The Puckerbrush Review.*

First Printing August, 1982
Second Printing November, 1982
Third Printing June, 1983
Fourth Printing July, 1984
Fifth Printing July, 1985
Sixth Printing June, 1986
Seventh Printing January, 1987
Eighth Printing February, 1988
Ninth Printing July, 1989
Tenth Printing November, 1990
Eleventh Printing October, 1994
Twelfth Printing November, 1997
Thirteenth Printing, February, 2002
Fourteenth Printing May, 2004

ISBN 0-913006-27-0

Printed in the United States of America
by Gossamer Press, Old Town, Maine
Bound by Furbush-Roberts Printing Company, Bangor, Maine

CONTENTS

INTRODUCTION

IN THE EARLY 1960s at the University of Maine there was this fellow in Sophomore Advanced Composition who kept writing stories about what seemed to be his relatives and neighbors down on the coast somewhere. Usually I had my students read their work aloud to the class (unless I had found it almost impossible to read to myself), and when Sanford Phippen read his, I soon learned to watch for a subtle change of expression among some of my students. They didn't exactly grin; there was on their faces just the beginning of a quiet, affectionately amused expression. They were the ones, I later figured out, who had grown up in rural Maine, inland or coastal. The others (I refuse to write that worn-out phrase, "from away," except in this parenthesis), from urban rather than rural communities, were interested, appreciative, but there was something they were missing (no fault of theirs): the pleasures of deep-rooted recognition.

Part of it, of course, was Sanford Phippen's voice, intonation, the genuine article, which self-conscious imitators almost always exaggerate, and thereby distort. But it was also, perhaps even more so, the genuine phraseology and diction of his characters' speech, neither absurdly extreme, nor colorlessly flat, that touched home with them.

A year later, Phippen turned up in a class of mine on the teaching of English in Secondary School (as if anyone knew exactly how one should do that!). Then, following graduation, he proceeded to do those two things: teach English in high school, and write.

One part of the result of that second activity is before you in this book. As reader, you will become acquainted with many people of Taunton, Maine, and environs, and you will do so by listening in on their dialogues. They talk a great deal, a trait which Phippen makes use of to delineate character. They will tell you about each other, not to mention their neighbors, and in doing that always tell you something about themselves.

So come along, listen to Bunny Crowley, Sid Griffin, "An-day," and learn things (more, see and hear them) about the worm diggers, the fish factory workers, Fredonna who "gave up day-to-day living," Garland Coffin, Fat Moon, and Julie Lawson (who is in more ways than one truly from another country). All are not humorous, nor should they be so: there are tales of pathos; some are grim; and certain ones among them are trenchantly moving, among them, "Step-Over Toe-Hold," "Queers in the Woods," and "The Returned Native" (about Lillie, who shifted from Maine to Alaska, and explains why). These, along with others, will show what Sanford Phippen has found to be "The Maine That's Missing" from other published works.

Edward M. Holmes

PREFACE

"WHAT IS YOUR WORLD VISION?" asked my friend Muriel Connerton of Syracuse, after hearing me read a couple of my stories to her one late November night in Boston. "Even though I like your stories, I don't know these people," she said. I confessed to having no "world vision," as far as I knew, but simply a "self vision," or perhaps, a "regional vision." Like Sarah Orne Jewett, a fellow Mainiac, I realize one has "to know the world before one can know the village." But while that oft-repeated truism isn't any kind of world vision, it's a good guide. I had to leave Maine, my growing up area, when I was 22 and go to live and work in central New York for fifteen years, before I could begin to "know myself" and look back at Eastern Maine and my hometown to put the place and the people in some kind of perspective. As Flannery O'Connor said in one of her letters in *The Habit of Being*, ". . . to know oneself is to know one's region, it is also to know the world, and it's also, paradoxically, a form of exile from that world, to know oneself is above all to know what one lacks . . ."

If I hadn't left Eastern Maine, I might still have written, but I wouldn't have written the stories collected here just the way I did. The only thing my characters have in common here is their Eastern Maine heritage, and the fact that they all have lived, at one time or another, in the same general area. Needless to say, they are all versions of me. They are fictionalized composites of people from my life, seen through my eyes, some of whom I have known well and others whom I haven't really known at all. Obviously, they all have multi-other sides invisible to me. Some are totally made up. It's not the characters, anyway, about whom I'm trying to tell "the truth." It's the emotional and psychological "truth" of life in Eastern Maine, as I have known it, sensed it, and felt it that I'm after.

While Muriel Connerton doesn't know these people, I do — in my mind and heart and soul. I identify closely with them and I love them, in fact. I couldn't write this way about them if I didn't. To me, like people in real life, my characters are simply representatives of both the funny and the tragic, existing always together at the same time, and sometimes crossing over.

Again to quote from Flannery O'Connor, ". . . to have sympathy for any character, you have to put a good deal of yourself in him." So, here is my sympathetic, however limited and regional vision, my partial answer to my own question, "What's missing from Maine's literature?"

Sanford Phippen
Orono, Maine
1982

THE POLICE KNOW EVERYTHING

WHENEVER I'M DOWN HOME on the coast visiting with my mother on the weekends, I usually try to stop by and have a chat with my Aunt Bunny Crowley, Taunton Ferry's oldest living policewoman. At 75, and a widow for the past eleven years, Aunt Bunny lives alone with only her ornery, orange-colored, long-haired, and yellow-eyed tomcat named Henry. Three days a week she drives down to The Point, the summer colony, where she cooks and cleans house for the former Ambassador to Mozambique and his wife, who retired here to their summer home about ten years ago. Bunny gets her jollies mostly from talking on and listening to her CB radio, reading detective novels, and scandalous magazines. Her CB handle is "Pie Maker" and she does seem always to have the makings of a pie spread out on her sideboard and kitchen table whenever I come to call.

In 1975, in the wake of an epidemic of break-ins and robberies on The Point, Taunton Ferry organized the county's first volunteer police force; and Aunt Bunny has been a stalwart member and outspoken supporter ever since. "It's great fun being on the police and it's important work we do," says Aunt Bunny. Once a week, usually on Saturday night, she goes on patrol with another aunt of mine, who because of her mannish ways, we call "Uncle Inez"; or with one of the thirty-odd men on the force, including my older brother, Bobber. Bunny is very proud of her police uniform, cap, and badge and loves her late night adventures on patrol. They drive all over town in a plain green Plymouth Volare police car. "Uncle Inez," who is fifty-five or so and married to my Uncle Hod, the town road commissioner for the past forty-one years, does the driving as First Officer while Aunt Bunny as Second Officer keeps the log. They start out as soon as it gets dark and stay out until around one a.m., keeping in close radio contact with Harley Hudson, the police chief, and his wife Mildred who mans the radio.

Bunny notes down in her log the time they take off and the time they land; and throughout the evening, she puts down the time every place they visit. "It's very important to keep accurate records," says Bunny. "Our records might be confiscated some day by the State Police, you see, and they'd want to know what we'd been up to."

"So what happened the other night when you were out?" I asked during my latest visit.

"Nothing. Just routine. It was a dull night — it didn't even rain."

"No crime?"

"Well, someone stole a case of pop out of the grammar school, and Aunt Inez arrested some rich bitch from Chicago who was looking at the sunset."

"Who was that?"

"Oh, that old Mrs. Wilson from down on The Point. She was parked up by Young's Lumberama near the Taunton Bridge and so we pulled in behind her and went over to her and asked her what she thought she was up to. She was very offended and snapped, 'I've been stopping here and admiring the sunset over this bay for thirty years!' When she said that, I thought Aunt Inez would blow her stack. Inez told her that she was loitering on private property and that she'd better get a move-on or be run in by the Taunton Police. Well, she gave us this snooty look, but she drove off. And that made Inez feel real good."

At this point, I tried to pick up Henry to pet him, but he snarled at me and started scratching my hands. "That Henry's a ruthless creature!" said Bunny. "Watch out he don't bite ya. He'll be just as nice and purring and then he'll attack. He's treacherous. Last night I thought he wanted some food, so I went to the refrigerator and he started chewing my ankles. He wanted to go out. Henry has a mind of his own, don't ya, Henry? He's just as sneaky as that awful Calvin Hayes and the Greels."

"What do you mean?"

"Well, we police spend most of our time trying to track 'em down. They're always up to something. The other night Inez and I were on patrol down on The Point when we come upon Calvin and The Greels.

Calvin left off school, ya know, and he's always up to no good, running with those awful Greels. Well, I went right up to 'em and gave 'em merry old hell. 'You'll have to go to the cooler!' I told that Calvin. They said they were just cutting blowdowns, but I knew better. Cripes! They were cutting trees off other people's land and selling the wood. And that Calvin Hayes, struttin' around just like a little cock bantam."

"Isn't he the blonde boy in the red sports car who flooded the tennis courts last summer?"

"Yeah. That's him. Always up to no good. Harley calls him The Prince of Darkness. He has a twisted brain. He used to read backwards. If only we could catch him in the act."

"How did you get to be a cop, Aunt Bunny?"

"Took courses at the high school, the court house, and down to Bar Harbor. I got two certificates. I've got the Miranda card right here in my purse. We had a meeting some time ago with the Hamlin Police. They just organized a force; but they can't carry guns. Now, jeepers creepers, I don't call that much of a force! You see a gun strapped on a guy and you know he's out for business."

"The other night we had the annual police meeting and Inez got to hooting and hollaring, as usual. We were electing officers, and she kept yelling, 'Doubt it!' Harley and Mildred were very upset over her remarks. And it was awful because Harley and Mildred have been very dedicated in their police work."

"Does Inez want to be the police chief?"

"Probably, but she mostly just hoots and hollars and no one listens to her. The men won't even go out with her, so I have to. I haven't seen her as mad as last year when she failed her gun test.

"I'd like to get the chance to go out with the men more. Chet Johnson is like going out with a big collie dog . . . and when you're with Bill Beal, you have to watch out. He heads right for the ditch!"

"What's it like going out with brother Bobber?"

"Oh, it's just like a circus with Bobber. He'll go anywhere and do anything. He likes to flash the lights around the harbor and into people's windows."

"Don't you think that borders on invasion of privacy?"

"Oh, no. The police crew are a dedicated bunch. And it's hard work. Listen, after five hours or more of trying doors all over town, telling people to move their cars out of the road, and taking down suspicious number plates, you do get worn out. Cripes, that's probably what the matter was with me the night I set off the alarm up at the machine shop at the Junction. That certainly caused a commotion. Inez yelled at me, 'Bunny, what in hell have you done!' "

"What was the most exciting thing that happened to you and Inez when you were out on patrol?"

"Well, last summer, Inez and I were patrolling up in North Taunton and there right in the middle of Route One there was a mess of hippies laying right in the road with their luggage. We almost run over 'em! We didn't stop, though, because Inez was scared. You know, despite all her big talk, Inez isn't as bold as she thinks she is. We drove right up to Harley's to tell him to move 'em. He took 'em down the other side of the Taunton Bridge and dumped 'em. I think they come from Boston Common.

"Then, there was that awful night last November when we got a call that Debbie Franklin had run off the road and smashed up her car. Her head got stove up pretty bad since it went through the windshield.

"Then, there's always some fracas going on at the trailer park."

"It does seem like you get all over town and get to know everybody."

"Sure we do. The police know everything. We have to. You never know what's going to happen next. Did you hear about all the trouble we've been having with Streaker Sargent?"

"No."

"Well, several weeks ago, he tried to make a date with Avis Trembley through the drive-up window at the Union Trust Company. And just recently, when Avis was house-sitting for the minister, Streaker started driving up there every night and parking in the driveway in his pick-up. Avis called the police and we told him he'd better stop bothering her. He also had a fire with his ever-bearing strawberries. Remember how he used to keep 'em in that glass case in the front window with that unnatural light on 'em?"

"Yes."

"Well, there was bad wiring or something for they caught on fire and burnt up the drapes and half the wall.

"I went patrolling with Harley one night and that was a lot of fun. We were up at the town dump when we came upon one of the Greels' vans parked mysteriously off to the side of the dump road. We sat there and waited, and by and by they come out of the bushes, hauling wood. They said they was just shooting raccoons, but we knew better, especially since seeing all the nice wood stacked up by the van. We watched them a while longer, but they didn't do anything except smoke cigarettes and talk. But you knew something was up. It's awful hard to catch 'em in the act, though. Harley's always saying to Inez and me, 'You haven't got another Greel you're going to bring in, are ya?' The Greels steal what they need. You can't get ahead of 'em. There'll always be Greels, for they're good breeders."

"Wasn't Calvin Hayes with them that night?"

"Nope. We caught him down by the town wharf in a car. Inez went up to 'em and there were these two boys, including Calvin, and a girl in the back seat. They were all slaphappy and Inez said, 'Who's driving this car?' They all just giggled and mimicked her, saying, 'I don't know — have we got a driver?' "

"Just who are all the people on the police force anyhow?"

"Oh, I can't tell ya that. The bad people might find out. That's why we have to use code numbers, too."

"But, Aunt Bunny, you can't have a secret police force in a democracy."

"You have to if you have secret criminals!

"Last Halloween, ya know, Inez almost got killed in the line of duty. Ruby Greel tried to run her down up on the East Side. Cripes, Inez was bouncing right up and down she was so mad! You see, we were chasing Ruby because she had stole some pumpkins; and as we were driving by, one of the Greel boys threw a pumpkin and an old pail which hit the police car. Inez got out to confront 'em, when that Ruby stepped on the gas and came driving right down the road after her. Inez had to jump in the ditch and you should have heard her cuss! She says she won't rest until she sees all of those goddam Greels locked up some place; but if I was her, I'd watch out. They're bad people. They came down one night last summer, ya know, and pulled up all of Inez's peas and made ruts in her lawn. They were warning her, I think."

"I just hope the police don't become vigilantes."

"Nope. We're just honest citizens trying to protect our property and keep down the crime.

"I did tell 'em at the annual meeting that I'd probably be quitting the force pretty soon. I'm too old and deaf to keep it up. But I guess I can't quit while Inez's still interested. She wouldn't have anyone to go on patrol with, since there always has to be two, and none of the men will go with her.

"Now, look at that foolish Henry." At this point, Henry had climbed into a bowl on the coffee table for his night's rest; and that's when I decided to make my exit. Upon my return home, my mother asked me if I had been enjoying all of Bunny's "cops and robber stories." I told her yes and about the Halloween caper with the Greels. All she said was, "It's just like a fairy story, An-day; it's so ridiculous."

IN SEARCH OF A SOLUTION

EVERY TWO WEEKS, Nellie Sawyer, who used to operate her own Cut 'n Curl shop right off Route One in North Taunton, but who now only makes house calls, would drive down to Taunton Ferry, about three miles down on Taunton Peninsula off the main road, in her Rabbit to keep a hair appointment with Sid Griffin and Bunny Crowley, two widowed sisters who had grown up and lived most of their lives in the same neighborhood.

Nellie's a tall, good-looking, and good-natured woman who wears glasses and has salt-and-pepper colored hair. On her calls she always wears her beauty operator's polyester blue smock, white slacks, and white nurse shoes. She always carries her black case of curlers, shampoos, solutions, bath towels, scissors, neutralizers, combs, and other assorted beauty equipment, and her hair dryer with her.

I used to be home sometimes during these beauty parlor sessions, puttering around in and out of the kitchen, and I'd overhear some of the conversations.

Since the women have been friends since grammar school, the three of them usually begin their familiar ritual sitting around Sid's kitchen table, which is also the dining room table, and have coffee and doughnuts or homemade coffee cake; and gossip. This one morning in late fall, Nellie just had to have two pieces of Sid's coffee cake.

"My God, Sid, isn't that delicious cake? I shouldn't, but I'm going to have another piece. What's your secret?"

"Oh, that's just a new recipe I got out of the *Grit* magazine. You use substitute eggs."

"Yes," said Bunny. "Sid gets 'em from phony hens!"

"Well, it's the best coffee cake I've had since that delicious one Inez's friend Claire had for the women's club open house. Remember how everyone was praising Claire for it?"

"Yes," said Bunny, "but what I remember best about that afternoon was Claire's telling us how she had had eight kids, and how seven had been home deliveries."

"No, is that right?" Nellie asked. "That Claire's quite a rugged gal, ain't she?"

"She'd have to be to be friends all this time with Inez," said Bunny.

"Say," said Nellie, "what's this I hear about Inez's quitting the police force?"

"Oh, she's just having one of her regular spells," said Bunny.

"Yes, she never sticks with anything," said Sid. "That's her pattern. She'll get all involved with one project, and then, all of a sudden, she has a big scene, or a blow-up with somebody, and quits!"

"Don't you drive with her on the police, Bunny?" asked Nellie.

"I used to, but we haven't been on patrol for more than a month. I miss it, because we have a lot of fun some nights. Harley Hudson, you know, he's the police chief. Well, Harley said I could go out with him now that Inez's quit; but cripes, he stays out till three a.m.; and that's too late for a great-grandmother like me."

"Well, I should say so," said Nellie, winking at Sid. "Well, girls, we might as well begin to git ya all fixed up, so you'll look extra beautiful for beano on Saturday night."

Sid removed the cake, coffee, cups, and spoons and started picking up, while Nellie got Bunny set up to have her hair colored. Both sisters were actually white-haired, but while Sid let hers be natural, Bunny had hers dyed red.

Since this particular early November morning they were both having permanents, a long process ensued. Nellie had to put the color on Bunny first, which had to stay on for a while and then be "washed out" before the trim and set. After the curlers are on, a solution is applied for the set. Then the hair has to be rinsed with cold water and the neutralizer applied. It's rinsed again, the curlers are taken out, the hair is washed one more time. Then, it's set and dried in the dryer. For the final step, it's combed out.

"O.K., Sid, Bunny's got her color on. I'm ready to shampoo ya," said Nellie. Bunny, with one of Nellie's bath towels wrapped around her, went to sit in the rocking chair by the front window, while

Nellie stuck Sid's head under the faucet in the kitchen sink in the pantry.

Upon returning to the kitchen proper, Nellie made Sid sit in one of the chairs by the table so she could begin to comb and trim her hair before rolling it and putting some solution on. At this point, the conversation about Inez and the police force continued.

"Bunny, anything interesting happen the last night you were out on patrol?" asked Nellie, who loved getting Bunny going on her stories.

"Well, let's see. There was this pregnant woman walking with a horse down Route One from North Taunton to Town Hill down on Mount Desert. She was leaving her husband, she said, and all she took was the horse. This was about ten p.m. and it reminded me of stories ya read about these women and men going across the country in western days. She was one of these hippy gals that has gone back to the land and who lived in the woods. She had a long dress and boots on. It was a queer sight in the middle of the night."

"Did you do anything to her?"

"Nope. Soon as we got her story, and I wrote it down in the log, we let her go. That same night, incidentally, Nellie, in your part of town, up in North Taunton again, there was this man we come upon sleeping in a station wagon. We found out later that he got evicted from his trailer at Taunton Heights. We thought, though, at the time he might have a woman in there with him. He was all wrapped up in the back seat, and it was dark and hard to tell, so we drove up to Harley's house to see him about it. Harley always says, 'When I send you women out, you run into the damndest things. Nobody else.' I just tell him that we're super cops!"

"Anything else going on in my part of town that I'm not aware of?" asked Nellie.

"Probably. There are bad people lurking everywhere, Inez says; but that last night we were out, I only remember people with flashlights sneaking around the golf course looking for night crawlers or mushrooms that glow in the dark or something. The rest of that night, in fact, all over town, the only other significant happening was a light on down at The Point, at Bowman's little cottage back of the big house. We called Harley on the radio and Mildred, his wife, called Sid. Ain't that right, Sid?"

"Yes," said Sid. "One of the workmen who was replacing the tiles on the floor had left a light on."

"O.K., Bunny, get ready now," said Nellie. "I got Sid rolled up. Now, it's your turn, just as soon as I put the solution to her." After Sid's curlers were all dabbed with the solution, the sisters exchanged places and continued their discussion.

"So, how come Inez quit the force?" Nellie asked. "What made her take such a drastic measure?"

"She didn't want the police to invite the selectmen to the annual police picnic this year," Bunny explained, "because she doesn't like Hank Tibbets, the first selectman."

"Oh?" Nellie asked. "Isn't he the one who wears a cowboy hat in the town office?"

"Yes, he's an evil man, Inez thinks. Anyway, we always have the picnic on Labor Day weekend, ya know, and it's been customary the last seven years to invite the selectmen. Inez burst into my house just before this year's picnic, just a few weeks ago, and I reminded her that she was on the committee for the food. 'No, I ain't!' she hollared. I told her that she never opened her head at the meeting we had beforehand, so it was assumed she was still on the committee. 'They can either choose Hank Tibbets or me!' she said. What's so funny is that neither Inez nor Hank showed up at the picnic."

"That's so typical of her," said Sid. "She tried working with the men on the road once but claimed she hurt her back and had to leave off. She worked the beano games with her father when he ran them and then suddenly quit going. She worked up to the box factory and also the blueberry factory at Taunton Junction, and had blow-ups at both. She quit the historical society because she felt the summer people had too much say. She was an excellent town clerk for several years, but she ended up feuding with everyone. Remember when she was all excited to take charge of the senior citizens' program and drive the old people around? That lasted only a couple of weeks."

"She's got something against every one of the police now," said Bunny. "Teddy Burns, who lives almost across the road from her, he's on the police, and he loves to get Inez going. He always asks her, 'Have you seen any bad people today?' Just foolish stuff, but it gets her goat. The last night we were out, Teddy told Inez she could drop the police car off at his house, for his patrol was the next night, and she said, 'He can come over to my house and git it!' "

"She doesn't seem to have much of a sense of humor about herself, does she?" asked Nellie.

"Nope," said Bunny. "Harley's trying to get her back on the force. He asked her last Sunday if she'd direct traffic up to the Congregational Church, but he had forgotten that she's a deacon now and goes to church every Sunday. 'I have to look after the whole church!' said Inez. Inez's a little afraid of Harley, however, since Harley is an ex-Marine. He played the trumpet in a parade in Washington, D.C., ya know."

"Oh?" asked Nellie, who by this time had finished rolling Bunny up, but who was now rummaging furiously through her black bag. "My God, I hope I brought that other bottle of solution! I can't seem to locate it. I know I took out a new bottle especially to bring. Oh, for Christ's sake!"

"What's the matter?" asked Sid, who was partially deaf, and rocking in the chair by the window while Bunny was in the chair by the table.

"Nellie can't find the solution, Sid!"

"Well, there's a little left in the old bottle that I used on Sid. Maybe, I can add a little water to it, and even if it's weaker, it'll be o.k."

"Well, I hope so," said Bunny. "I want this permanent to be permanent, ya know."

"Well, I've got plenty of neutralizer and other stuff, but by God, that's all the solution. Wouldn't ya know! Well, Bunny, if it don't work the way it should, I'll do ya over again next week for free."

"You're damned right, you will, Nellie."

After Nellie left that day, Bunny said, "Sid, it gets worse every time, doesn't it?"

"It does seem as if she does something wrong every time," Sid agreed. "Last time she slopped the coloring on the floor and now there are those two dark spots on my rug. I don't think she sees as well as she used to, and she's always rushing things."

"She shakes all over," said Bunny. "Maybe she's got the palsy or something. Do you want to call her and tell her not to come next time?"

"No. Who else could we get? You don't want to drive all the way into Ellsworth, do you?"

"No. The good thing is she's handy and convenient and she comes to us. Let's wait a while, until she really screws up. If our hair starts falling out, we'll have to find someone else."

THE PROBLEMS OF HISTORICAL RESEARCH

THERE'D BEEN A MINI-FAMILY REUNION at the Hilltopper Lounge in honor of Aunt Sid's sixty-fifth birthday. Uncle Oliver had paid for his and Aunt Bunny's dinners. I'd paid for Sid's and mine. That hadn't been the plan; but that's how it worked out. In the parking lot afterwards, shy bachelor Uncle Oliver reluctantly posed between his two sisters for an Instamatic photo or two. I, the dutiful nephew, played photographer.

"You're a senior citizen now, Sid," said Bunny. "You can get free meals and into the movies for a dollar. It's just like being a kid again."

Sid made no reply. She just said, "Hurry up, An-day. I hate to have my picture taken."

"You ought to go get your hair dyed like mine," said Bunny. "Then you wouldn't mind so much."

"You've ruined your hair with that rinse; and it's not even natural," said Sid. "Your hair was never red like that."

"Who wants to be natural?" Bunny looked at me and winked.

"I've got to be going," said Uncle Oliver.

"O.K.," I said. "I've gotcha on film; you are excused."

"That's right, Ollie; get back in your cage," said Bunny. "Lemme know if you want another apple pie next Sunday or not." Bunny cooked and washed for Oliver.

Oliver drove off in his new, plain green Plymouth that had been a "demonstrator model" to the caretaker's cottage the other side of Ellsworth where he lived and worked alone with only an old guard dog for company. While we — Aunts Sid and Bunny and I — got in Sid's bright blue Chevette for the drive back home; but on our way Bunny suggested we stop at the Bird Sanctuary.

"Have you ever seen it?" she asked.

"No, but I've always wanted to," I said.

"What?" asked Sid, who was deaf; and because of this remained very reticent with a vacant grin on her face.

"The bird sanctuary, Sid!" Bunny hollared to Sid in the back seat. "Don't you want to stop and examine the horny owls?"

"That might be nice," said Sid.

We didn't stop long, only to sign our names in the guest book, make a dollar donation, wander down one path through the woods and around a pond where some ducks and geese were squabbling. Then we peered into the cages where there were various types of Maine owls and one old crow.

"I hear they have to feed a mouse a day to these feathered beasts," said Bunny. "Poor things aren't able to catch their own any more. I wonder who captures the mice for 'em?"

"What?" asked Sid.

Back in the Chevette, the sisterly conversation continued while I drove.

"Remember that evil hawk that killed all our chickens at home on the farm that time, Sid?" asked Bunny.

"I guess probably," Sid said. "Almost wiped us out one spring."

"It was right after that March night when Zelda lost her baby," said Bunny. "I remember because it seemed like everything went to hell that year."

"What baby did Aunt Zelda lose?" I asked. "I never knew she lost one."

"Yes, it was born dead — the first one, a boy. I had to wrap it up," said Bunny.

"Doctor Black couldn't get through because of the snowstorm," said Sid. "He could only get as far as Gallison's Corner and then the boys had to go out by horse and sled and get him."

"He stayed overnight," said Bunny, "and it's just as well since Eller almost died that night, too."

"What happened to Aunt Eller?" I asked, anxious to know more about this awful night among my female relatives long before I was born.

"Oh, she had double pneumonia. Eller never wore no clothes, ya know. She just threw a dress on with nothing else underneath, even in the middle of the winter. Never took care of herself," said Bunny.

"What did Doctor Black do?" I asked.

"Handed out some pink pills," Sid said. "That's all they ever gave ya in those days — little pink pills."

"Probably full of heroin or some other dreadful drug," said Bunny.

"Did Grammie help deliver Zelda's dead baby?" I asked.

"Of course!" said Bunny. "Grammie was a certified Maine midwife."

"How do you get to be certified in that field?" I asked.

"Have twelve kids of your own like Grammie did!" said Bunny. "Grammie was an expert about havin' babies."

"Oh, it was a wild night that night. Eller dying in the little room off Grammie and Papa's room where Zelda was screaming and cussing the air blue. Grammie, who was a gentlewoman, was very upset over Zelda's swearing. Zelda could swear something wicked."

"What about Papa? Where was he?"

"Probably asleep. Papa tried hard, but he was never any good at housework," said Bunny.

"Papa swore, didn't he?"

"Papa never said anything but 'shit' in the house. He never said 'goddamn' in the house, but he did down in the barn," said Bunny.

"They were strict Baptists, remember," said Sid.

"Anyway, the next morning I had to tell Zelda she had a dead baby," said Bunny.

"What was her reaction?" I asked.

"She said, 'Well, goddamn it! I'll have another one next year!' She did, too. That was just the way Zelda was. She was from Cherryfield and they grow 'em tough down there," said Bunny.

"God, what a night. We didn't know which one was going to die first," said Bunny. "Aunt Pill and I took turns helping Grammie out so she could get some sleep."

"I don't know if you've got the story exactly right," said Sid. "Are you sure you aren't getting Zelda mixed up with Thelma? She had a dead baby, too, you know, about the same time."

"It was the season of the dead babies!" I said.

"Yes, Sid; but she didn't have it at home. Thelma's baby was brought home from Bangor and we buried it. I should know; I wrapped Zelda's dead baby up for burial. It was a nice looking little boy except for the head where when you tipped it up, you could see the big bag of water, swishing back and forth. Doctor Black said it probably didn't have any brain."

"I'm not sure you've got it right, that's all," said Aunt Sid.

"Sid, I'm ten years older than you! You were just a tyke, probably hiding under a bed upstairs! You were always such a queer dick."

"You're only *nine* years older and I think you're getting senile," said Sid.

"I dressed the baby in little baby clothes and Ira Johnson made a little casket for it. I took my son Joe's little cushion — it was his baby pillow — and put it in the casket. Aunt Pill helped me fix the casket up all nice."

"When was this exactly? What year?" I asked.

"Must have been around 1928 or so," said Bunny. "The so-called Roaring Twenties, because Joe was only about two years old."

"It was 1930," said Sid. "I was fifteen. I wasn't any little tyke. I remember the whole thing very clearly. And later on, Grammie confided a lot in me."

"Well, what I remember was coming home to my husband at five the next morning wading in that snow up to my waist. It was definitely March or February. When we get home I'll run in the house and check my little date book."

"It'll take more than a date book to clear up that fog between your ears," said Sid. "God, are you ever getting to be a crazy old woman."

"An-day, we'll just have to see about getting Sid a new hearing aid. She misses a lot of vital information the way she is now. It's a sad thing, really pathetic."

"I'm no more deaf than you are, *Aunt Bunny!*" said Sid.

"You know, Morris and Leona had a dead baby, too, 'bout the same time as Zelda and Thelma," said Bunny.

"Let's not talk about dead babies any more. You're so morbid," said Sid.

"I'm notorious!" said Bunny. "But I love to go out on patrol with the police and learn all these gruesome things, instead of sitting home watching Lawrence Welk and feeling sorry for myself!"

"You're nuts!" said Sid.

"Sid, you've just been all upset ever since last week when we were having our hair done and I told Nellie that it was me who showed you how to put patchwork together."

"My God, Bunny; you have really gone around the bend! You *never* showed me how to put patchwork together! I learned how to do that when I went to Guild. I made a butterfly quilt once and Agnes Kief showed me how to do it. I also learned from watching old Mrs. Grant, who was a fine seamstress. Grammie told me I was the *one daughter* of hers who *knew how* to get things done! All you ever knew was how to milk a cow and that's about it!"

"Well, Sid's right about that one thing, An-day. I always loved to work down in the barn and outdoors with the men. It was much more fun than being cooped up in the house with grieving women like Grammie and Sid!"

"Well, Aunties, I'm confused. Was it Zelda who had the dead baby that awful snowy night, or not?"

"It doesn't matter, An-day," said Bunny. "It's all in the past. I did have to sit up with Zelda and give her ether, though."

"Doctor Black gave Zelda the ether, not you!" said Sid from the backseat.

"Oh, Sid, shut up and stop ruining my fun!" said Bunny.

BUNNY CROWLEY TAKES HER DRIVING TEST

THE LAW IN THE STATE OF MAINE decrees that by age 75, a driver, if he wants to renew his license, must take a road test. So my Aunt Bunny Crowley, who turned 75 last year, and who has driven cars and trucks all her life, found herself faced with the fact of having to take her first driving test.

Having worked on a farm, driven tractors and a milk truck, and chauffeured the summer people about Taunton Point for fifty years, as well as having driven in and around Philadelphia and Boston where she and Uncle Eugene worked as a maid-and-butler team for decades, it did seem as ludicrous an idea as asking Aunt Bunny to make an apple pie, another skill she had mastered early on in life.

"They send ya a book of rules just as if you're a newcomer," said Aunt Bunny. However, despite her characteristic bravado, she did place the rulebook right on her living room coffee table and studied it every night. She was nervous about the test, after all. "Everyone I know of has failed on their first try," said Bunny. "Look at Hanky Ray. He went around the corner too fast and a tire went up on the sidewalk. Of course, he and Bibben don't know their way around Ellsworth anyway. They know one way in and one way out. And, God, poor old Carrie. She practiced and practiced. She even borrowed her niece Trudy's car. But they get ya on the hill. You've got to know how to brake on a hill; and just because Carrie's car rolled a little bit on State Street Hill, they flunked her. She was so discouraged after that, she sold her car and now has to depend upon someone else to drive her into Ellsworth or anywhere else. I don't want to be like that. I want to be able to go when and where I want to as long as possible. I'm an independent cuss that way, ya know."

"I know," I said.

"I always thought it was real sad what happened to Fred Rand."

"What was that?"

"He didn't pass. Mildred went right over and begged them to get Fred a license just for use on Taunton Point. She said that was his only pleasure in his old age — driving around The Point. After supper every night, you used to see 'em going for a spin."

"They refused her?"

"Of course! And Fred died right after that."

"Well, I don't think your losing your license will kill you."

"No, but, cripes! It will be quite a calamity."

I left Aunt Bunny studying her rulebook that Sunday. She was scheduled to take her test that week. The next weekend I was home, watching an old movie on TV, when Bunny's red Pinto pulled in the driveway. Sid was out in the kitchen, and I hollared to her, "I take it Bunny passed her test."

"Yes, and now you're about to get the play-by-play description," said my mother.

Bunny burst through the kitchen door, which is our front door, as brusque and full of business as ever, her arms full of garments and a large pocketbook.

"Cripes!" she said, plopping the stuff down on the kitchen table in front of Sid, who had been sewing. "Lydia Adams has had her claws into me all week! And here are some more bothersome little chores that she'd like you to take on, Sid!"

"Oh, they're always so ridiculous," said Sid. "It seems like for Lydia I'm always sewing patches on top of patches."

"That's right. Lydia's a frugal one. She never throws anything away. Remember those ancient clothes from her mother's in Bangor that you had to sew some cloth on the bottom of so she could wear 'em?"

"Yes, and those narrow old ski pants that I had to put a piece in so she could wear'em to Sugarloaf. I just hope I won't have to repair that U.S. flag of theirs again this year."

"No, they're getting a new one."

"Good. Well, what are these jobs.?"

"She needs new zippers in this dress and this pair of slacks."

"O.K."

"Now, here's a towel that needs patching."

"My God."

"How about this old handbag where the cotton shows through? Can you fix that?"

"No. I can't repair that. The dress, pants, and the towel, but not the pocketbook. She must think I'm some kind of miracle worker. I can't do work on plastic and leather."

"Well, she's never forgotten that time you fixed her Woman's Fire Auxiliary yellow jacket. That was made out of some unnatural substance. Remember how hers wouldn't come together right and you fixed it so it would?"

"Yes."

At this point I got up from my spot in front of the TV, walked out into the kitchen and interrupted the conversation.

"So, Aunt Bunny, I'm dying to hear. Did you pass your driver's test or not?"

"Well, of course! Didn't you think I would?"

"Yes, I certainly knew you'd make a strong impression, one way or the other."

We both sat down at the kitchen table; and Sid said, "I'll go get the coffee. I've also got some date crumbles and blonde brownies to go with it."

"So what happened exactly?" I asked. Any story from Aunt Bunny was apt to be good, since she was a natural-born yarn-spinner; but an occasion like one's first driving test at 75 was special. Aunt Bunny was one of those people who could make driving to Ellsworth to get groceries sound as adventurous and daring as crossing the Himalayas.

"I did everything everyone told me to do," said Bunny. "I cleaned the car. Inez went with me, but she didn't want to. She wanted to be in Portland where they were having this Christian women's convention last week; but Uncle Hod wouldn't let her go."

"Is that how Inez sees herself nowadays — a Christian woman?"

"Oh, yes. She became born again as soon as they made her a deacon at the church. I think that was part of the deal."

"Back to the driving test."

"Yes, well, first I had to go to the optometrist's, and as luck would have it, my new lens was in. Had to have the full report on my eyeballs, ya see. Now, I can see all kinds of distances. I can even see sideways. I can look at you and then right out the window without any problem. But, cripes! Fifty nine dollars just for that piece of glass!"

She continued. "Well, then I went over to the city hall down in the basement. There was a young fella there and I asked him if he was seventy-five. I was scared to death that I was going to get that picky old grump that flunked Hanky, Carrie, and Fred; but I lucked out again. I got a nice young man. I just took my time and looked all around. He said, 'Start 'er up and let 'er idle.' He was just as calm and collective all the time. I was worried about my little old Pinto. She's ten years old, ya know. She's getting on. And if you fumble with ya gears, you're done for. I kept saying, 'Listen, old girl, don't you stall on me!' "

"So, what was the route? Did you have to brake on State Street Hill?"

"No! It was simple as pie. No one-way streets, no hills, and no lights. There wasn't even much traffic. Ya know, when I was practicing beforehand, my son Merle said, 'Ma, your biggest fault is you don't stop at stop signs.' I told him that I'll stop fifteen minutes if I have to!"

"You did have stop signs?"

"Yes, and he also made sure I used my signal lights a lot. But I didn't go up on the sidewalk or run anyone down. Didn't have any head-on collisions. When we got back to the city hall parking lot, he told this other cop, 'She's a good driver.' "

"How long have you had a license, Aunt Bunny?"

"1924 — fifty-eight years. I didn't want to tell 'em because they might think she's no good now! In fact, I thought I'd better not say anything at all, afraid he'd be hard on me."

"Well, you did all right. Congratulations."

"Thanks. Now all I've got to do is go have my teeth looked at."

FIRE DOWN IN THE BACK FIELD

IT HAPPENED IN EARLY JUNE after school one afternoon, when it had been an especially dry spring, that my cousin, Buster Partridge, set the field down back of his parents' house on fire. He didn't mean to; he was about nine at the time and liked to play with matches.

His older sister Lovina, just off the schoolbus, ran into the front room where Aunt Eller, as was her customary afternoon habit, lay dozing with a beer and the *Police Gazette.* She was almost asleep when Lovina started yelling, "Mama! The back field's on fire!"

Aunt Eller's feet kicked the air for about five minutes before she could upright herself, get her loafers on, and make a mad dash to the back of the house, out through the shed, where she grabbed a broom, and down to the back field, where she started beating out the blaze. But there was a breeze, and the fire was quickly spreading through the field near the barn out beyond the chicken coops, and down into the woods.

"Go git Aunt Inez!" Eller yelled at Lovina, who jumped on her bike and started down the road. None of the menfolk were at home from work at this time of day; but Inez, as Eller knew, was very active in the newly-formed volunteer fire department and had driven the new red truck. Inez would at least know who to contact and call up.

When Lovina, peddling like crazy, came racing into Aunt Inez' driveway, she ran into Albert Collingswood, a scruffy town character who did odd jobs down on The Point, and who was then sitting on the running board of his old beat-up pick-up, smoking a cigarette.

"Where's Inez?" asked Lovina in a flurry.

"What's the trouble, little gal?" asked Albert, who appeared always unshaven and in his undershirt.

"Our field is on fire! I want to get Aunt Inez to call the firemen!"

"Well, Jesus Christ, little woman! The first thing ya should do is ya gotta hollar fire!" And, at that point, he threw back his head and bellowed, "FIRE!"

"What good is that going to do," asked Lovina, "if there's no one within five miles to hear ya?"

"Well, ya can't tell. Somebody might."

"Oh, Albert, you're crazy!" she said, running into Inez' house, dragging her aunt off the phone and telling her about the fire.

"You call Gertie down to The Point!" said Inez. "Tell her to sound the alarm and call up to The Corner and alert everyone there. I'll go for the truck!"

Inez jumped into her car and peeled out of the driveway, sending up a cloud of dust that caused Albert, who was trying to blow his nose, to cough and sputter, "Christ Almighty!"

After calling Gertie, who set the alarm on The Point, Lovina got back on her bike and peddled like a bat out of hell back up the road, arriving on the scene just as her older sisters, Lillie and Kitty, were getting home from high school. Everyone was down in the back field with brooms, evergreen tree limbs, and pails and pans of water trying to put out the blaze, which was now spreading over the whole field heading towards the woods which surrounded the old farmstead.

Aunt Eller was concerned about the horse in the barn. "Lovina, git in the barn and git the horse out! But be careful!"

I had just gotten home from school, too, like everyone else; and just as I was going into my house down the road, in the other direction from Aunt Inez' and Aunt Eller's, I heard the fire alarm sounding from down on The Point. And it wasn't long before all of us were running down the road to the Partridge's where we could now see the smoke billowing above the trees from the back field.

When I got there, it was just like every other fire I had ever known in our Taunton Ferry neighborhood over the years.

When the town finally got around to buying a new fire truck, and organizing the Volunteer Fire Department, the truck was treated like a shiny, new toy. Everyone got a chance to turn on the si-reen and have a ride around town in it. A new garage was built at Taunton Corner to house it. Many could hardly wait for the first blaze to test out the new equipment.

They got the chance one cold spring night when Clint Wooster had a chimney fire. However, coming down the west side of Taunton

Peninsula from Taunton Corner, young Junior Moon was driving like a madman, the si-reen going full of blast; but Junior forgot that in the spring, Taunton's roads are full of frost heave and this spring it was especially bad. The truck bounced and jounced all over the place, and by the time Junior pulled up Clint's driveway, and the flames were shooting out of the chimney, some of the pipes under the truck had gotten broken or something, since only a trickle of water could be forced out of the hose. Thus, the truck wasn't any help and the fire had to be fought by hand.

Clint's getting very senile, and right in the middle of the fire fighting, he was out on the front porch inviting everyone in for coffee. At one point, Junior, who seemed to be everywhere that night — a regular savior of men — ran upstairs with his fireman hat on and started ripping the wallpaper off the wall in the bedroom over the kitchen. It was true that the fire was in the kitchen chimney, but it took a while for people out on the lawn to shout at Junior and make him realize that he was ripping the paper off the wrong wall.

I was present in the throng that night, having been across the road chatting with a neighbor girl, Helen Springer, who was home on vacation from her sophomore year at the University of Maine. Helen was chuckling wildly to herself throughout the whole scene, persuading me to race back to her house to get a note pad and pen with which she could take some notes. "This is just the type of stuff I need for an A essay in Advanced Writing," she told me. By the time I got back, someone had set up a table with coffee and sandwiches for the firemen; and it seemed like the whole town was there. People had brought blankets and were talking over their CB radios. My Aunt Inez was helping old Margaret Carter across the lawn so she could get a closer look at the blaze. "Is it bad? Is it bad?" she kept asking Inez, who said, in her usual gruff manner, "The house hasn't burned down, Margaret! Look up! Look up at the chimney, and you'll see the fire! There it is — see!"

Members of the Woman's Fire Auxiliary made sure everyone got a cup of coffee and a doughnut. Some people were sitting in their cars wrapped up in their blankets; and, finally, the chimney fire was put out. Junior Moon, the hero, was covered with soot from head to toe.

But back to the fire in the field.

By the time I got down to my aunt's that bright, windy afternoon, the fire was definitely out of control and into the woods. At one point, I remember seeing my Cousin Lillie rushing down the field with a plastic dishpan full of water and suds, which, when a small tree beside her suddenly went up in a roar of flames, she tossed into the air. She screamed and ran back, not bothering to rescue the pan.

Sadly, little Buster came running up to me, crying and blubbering about how he didn't mean to start it. He held in his hands a glass of water which he was going to throw on the fire. "The wind's going about seven hundred miles an hour now," he said, "and everything's going to burn up!"

Aunt Eller hollared at Buster, "Go tie up the dog and git him out of the way!"

Off in the distance we could hear the si-reen of the fire truck getting nearer and nearer to the Ferry as it raced down the east side of the peninsula. In seconds it appeared with Inez, smoking a cigarette and looking like Johnny Cash, at the wheel. She had three or four teenage boys about my age with her and a half-dozen Indian pumps. They filled up the pumps with water from the truck and strapped one of them on my back. I nearly fell over; that pump must have weighed a hundred pounds. "You go down that way and start spraying!" Fire Chief Inez ordered. I could barely run with that tank on my back, but I managed to stumble along through the field, spraying as I went, but the smoke was awful; and it frightened me how fast the trees caught on fire and burned. I came back and forth several times to get my pump refilled; and each time I looked around, there were more and more people, and another fire truck from nearby West Hamlin. There was a natural spring and a small swamp down in the middle of the woods which helped slow down the fire and replenish the water supply. Eventually, the blaze was put out, after burning only a few acres. None of the livestock nor buildings were lost and no one was hurt, beyond exhaustion and some smoke inhalation. The Woman's Fire Auxiliary arrived with coffee, soda pop, and sandwiches; and a number of neighbors stood around talking. Aunts Eller and Inez were both smoking their cigarettes.

"Ya know," said Eller, "I put those matches up high enough so I didn't think he could reach 'em."

"It isn't your fault," said Inez. "Kids can always git to the matches."

"No, but God, I've always been scared of fire, ever since Ellsworth burnt flat back in the thirties; and that awful week in 1947 when Bar Harbor burned. The sky was red around here for nights. And some of the awful house fires we've had in this town."

"Next to death," said Aunt Inez, "there's nothing worse than losing your house and everything ya own."

A picture news story of Inez seated in the fire truck made headlines the next day in the Bangor *Daily News* and was later picked up by the Associated Press and printed across the country. My mother,

Aunt Eller, and the neighbors were all tickled to read how the Los Angeles *Times*, as well as one of the Chicago papers, described Aunt Inez, who had always driven trucks and liked to work on the road with the men, as a "petite Maine housewife."

"It was a good thing she was at home," said Aunt Eller. "Otherwise, I'd have lost my chickens, the horse, the barn, and probably the whole forest. Ya gotta hand it to Inez. She wheeled that truck right in and around here like nobody's business. And she ordered everyone around like a real fire chief, no thanks to all the brave men in town who evidently were busy taking an extended lunch break, which reminds me — whatever happened to Albert Collingswood?"

"Oh, he's probably still sitting down to Inez's on his truck hollaring, 'FIRE!' into the wind," said Lovina.

SISTER'S WEDDING HAD A LOT OF FIRSTS

I HAD NEVER SEEN SID SO RILED ABOUT ANYTHING. My cousin and her niece, Sister Partridge, was about to be married; and for weeks prior to the event, Sid ranted and raved about how insane the whole affair was becoming.

"I'm not going! That's all there is to it!" said Sid.

"But you've got to go," I said. "After Aunt Eller died, you practically brought Sister up."

"Well, you can go if you want to, but as far as I'm concerned she's gone too far now."

"What do you mean?"

"She sent out some invitations to the wedding to some of the relatives and some just to the reception for others. She's split up whole families."

"Isn't that typical?"

"No. Not the way she did it. It just causes hard feelings. She didn't even send Buster, her own brother, an invitation. I called her on that, and she said it was her wedding and she was going to have it her way or not at all. I told her, 'Sister, this isn't right what you've done. You should have either invited everybody or no one.' "

"What did she say to that?"

"She said she thought more of her friends than most of her relatives anyway."

"Well, God knows that's true."

"Well, I'm fed up with her. I certainly don't want to go to her hillbilly wedding!"

"Why do you call it that?"

"Because that's exactly what it is. She met him at the Holiday Inn Bar. She's been living with this guy for four or five months and now she's got nerve enough to go into a church and be married in a white wedding gown."

"She isn't the first one in this town to do that. Maybe she's just copying her sister Spunky? I remember Spunky living out in the woods with that gang of woodchoppers before she got hitched. And before that she was in love with a drag strip racer and took up car racing. Remember that picture of her in the Bangor *Daily News* standing in the grease pit at the Unity Raceway? Spunk was something else in her time, and Sister always took after her."

"Yes, that's true; but Sister's tougher than Spunky ever was."

"Well, that's how it looks now from this angle. Say, who is this guy Sister's marrying, anyhow?"

"All I can say is he gets up in the morning and goes to work. He works in the woods."

"Well, that's something."

"He was also picked up recently for speeding and fined fifty dollars."

"Well, that doesn't necessarily signify much either."

"It's still just like a backwoods wedding if you ask me. You should have seen Sister at the shower the girls here in the neighborhood gave her last week."

"Tell me about it."

"She had on a straw hat with a feather in it and jeans on. She didn't even take the hat off. All she wanted was money to go on *The Bluenose* for her honeymoon. She kept saying she wanted to get pregnant right away — get it over with. She had lovely wedding gifts really. They were too good for her. She had some of his womenfolk with her and I never did get introduced to any of 'em. They looked like people from way out in the woods somewheres. They say his mother is forcing the whole thing to make her settle him down; but I bet ya from what I've been hearing they'll both be plastered at the wedding."

"Well, that won't be the first time that's happened either. When I used to play the organ at the church, and for many shotgun weddings, I remember most of those affairs as being well-oiled. No one seemed to be listening too intently to the sacred vows."

"Well, that's what I'm talking about. I don't want to see Sister having a drunken, awful wedding ceremony like that. I want her to have a nice and decent one."

"Is the wedding going to be here in Taunton?"

"Yes. At the Congregational Church, but the reception is to be some place else. We don't have a hall here that's good enough. She came bursting through the door just last week, hollaring, as she always does, 'I'm hungry! Feed me!' — as if she needed any extra pounds. In one breath she told me how she had had her car repossessed, probably due to lack of payments, and how she was taking her case to the D.A. and to the Small Claims Court. And in the next breath, she told me about all her big wedding plans, how she's going to have six tuxedos and a two-hundred-and-fifty-dollar orchestra. She doesn't want to hold the reception in the Taunton Town Hall, because, as she says, 'that floor wouldn't hold up what I'm having.' "

"So, who's going and who's not?"

"Well, Yvonne said that she and Merle, who are first cousins after all, were members of the church and so they could go anyway, even if Sister didn't invite them. And Buster dropped by the other day and said he was going. He did say, though, that because Sister owed him some money he was going to deduct it from his wedding gift. All the Partridge aunts, of course, will be down from Bangor for the occasion."

"All I ever remember over the years seeing them is how they'd show up together, huddle together while here, never speaking to any of us, and then leave together. They'd always be wearing new polyester pants suits and high heel shoes to complement their bee-hive hairdos and plucked black eyebrows and dangling earrings. They'd always be perpetually scowling, smoking their cigarettes off in some corner, gossiping together as if in some conspiracy against the rest of us."

"They're awful snobs, and they all have long and colorful histories."

"I bet. What about Hanky and Bibben? Is Hanky going to give Sister away, since he's the only surviving uncle?"

"Yes, they've been back and forth about that, too; but Hanky finally consented. He is her uncle, after all. Of course, Bibben is going all out and buying an expensive new gown for the occasion. She's made at least two trips already to Bangor to find one. Bibben would be a snob, too, but she doesn't know how."

"So, it sounds like everything's shaping up."

"I don't know, and I don't care. I just think the whole thing is a disgraceful affair and I don't want any part of it. She's ruined it for me."

"I think you're being a little hard on Sister. Look at how she's grown up. After Aunt Eller died, when she was just a little kid, and then living with Uncle Fod in that trailer with his constant drinking bouts every weekend. And being with him alone when he died. She's had a tough time all her life."

"Well, she's not improving her situation any with this farce of a wedding."

"How do you know? I think all we can do is lend our support, love her, and give her our best."

Even though I tried, I couldn't convince my mother at that point that she should attend Sister's wedding; but during the week while I was in Orono teaching, an incident occurred involving the wedding cake which brought Sid back into the fold. As my Cousin Lovina later explained it to me, "Aunt Sid was just all upset because Sister didn't let her plan the whole wedding; but once Sid got to make the cake she felt more involved with the operation and softened in her feelings towards Sister."

"So tell me all about the wedding cake," I said when I got home the next weekend, the big weekend of Sister's nuptials.

"There are just no words to describe this wedding," she began. "Sister had arranged to have this fancy cake made by some of her big-deal, so-called friends over in Ellsworth; but she was more concerned about getting the camper washed for the honeymoon than the wedding cake made. Her mother-in-law-to-be told her she ought to call down and see about the cake. Well, she did, only to find out that her big friends let her down. They had forgotten all about it, so she came a-running and a-wailing to me at the last moment."

"What did you say?"

"I told her you can't make a wedding cake in one day; but that I'd see what I could do. Of course, she was always too busy to really help us. In fact, while Lovina and I were busy up at Lovina's trying to get the cake done, Sister put on her shorts and halter and was out washing the camper! She must have washed that camper ten times!"

"Well, she'll probably be that crazy way all her life. I don't see why you expect her to change just because she's getting married."

"I guess I don't. I'm just still so upset over the whole mess."

"You did get the cake made?"

"Yes, it's all ready and in the freezer over to Lovina's; but Sister doesn't like it because it's a little crooked. I told her she could just turn it around so the good side shows."

And so we did. But while only the good side of the cake showed, family relationships were revealed from every angle.

Sid did attend the wedding with me; and even the reception, and so did most of the rest of the relatives, invited or not.

Waiting there in the Congregational Church, the familiar scene of so many weddings, funerals, choir rehearsals, Christmas and Easter celebrations, and church ceremonies throughout my life, I watched the old pews filling up with the friends and relatives of the bride and groom. His people didn't really seem like hillbillies to me, but their clothes were a little cheaper made and shabbier than ours. Most of the men had on ill-fitting sport coats and white socks. There were no tuxedos in the wedding party.

I'll never forget the sight of Sister in her wedding gown on the arm of Uncle Hanky, standing there framed in the front entrance of the church just as the strains of "The Wedding March" had begun. Sister, a big, strapping girl, towered over her diminutive uncle. Both looked so serious and yet so funny, sort of yet another satirical version of "American Gothic," Downeast style.

During the straightforward ceremony, presided over by the first woman preacher of our church, a pretty blonde-haired young lady from Yale, there was only one jarring note: when the Reverend told someone in the congregation to stop taking pictures, while she proceeded with the rites. Also, the kiss bothered me, because it wasn't a kiss. It was a perfunctory peck.

At the reception, which was held in "The Culvert," the nearby Jefferson Town Hall, which is of the practical Quonset Hut design, and hardly as impressive as Taunton's stately Town Hall, the estrangement of families was complete. His people sat on one side of the hall and we sat on the other. As expected, the Partridge aunts with their impressively plucked eyebrows and cigarettes sat by themselves talking with Hanky and Bibben. There was no orchestra, only a small stereo for music. There was a gift table and another table for the punch, goodies, and the crooked wedding cake. There were a number of coolers off to one side packed with beer and wine. The spiked punch bowl was empty long before the plain punch bowl was even touched. No reception line was formed, so I had to go over to the groom and introduce myself. He had a weak handshake and seemed surprised that I would want to meet him. At one point a friend of the groom's proposed a toast and then made an announcement that the men present could dance with the bride for a dollar. Sid and I left early.

A few weeks after the wedding, I was talking to Aunt Bunny Crowley, who had been there, about it.

"What did you think of that wedding, Aunt Bunny?"

"Sister's wedding sure had a lot of firsts for me," she said. "That blanket thank-you to everyone that she had printed in the paper — that was the first time I'd seen anything like that. And at the reception having the men all pay a dollar to dance with her so they could pay for their honeymoon on *The Bluenose* — that was another first. It was really the queerest wedding I've ever seen, and I've seen some real beauts. She calls him 'that thing.' Somehow I don't think they married for love."

"Lovina said that after almost everyone had left the reception, this big yellow Cadillac pulled up outside and the strangers in it wanted to know if they could join the party."

"Well, I'm not surprised. There were things you never heard of at that wedding. Sister couldn't even keep her groom in the hall. He was always going off outdoors with his buddies."

"I haven't seen her since the wedding, have you?"

"Yes, just last week, I saw her at the checkout counter over to the IGA. She had about ten candy bars, some bottles of pop, a pound of margarine, and a big bag of potato chips. She and her husband, ya know, have both just lost their jobs; and I asked her what she was living on. 'Faith,' she said. And I said, 'Well, that's good. I don't have any of that.' "

THE DEATH OF A LOBSTER TRUCK DRIVER

THE NIGHT UNCLE FOD DIED, I thought the Princess phone was going to ring right off the wall. I had just gotten home from Syracuse for the summer; another long year of schoolteaching had come to an end; and I was looking forward to completing my research and chapters for the proposed Sesquicentennial Taunton town history book. I had just fallen asleep when the phone woke me up. Evidently it had been ringing for some time before I got downstairs; and because it was the middle of the night, I knew it must be some kind of emergency. Somehow the very ring sounded urgent. My mother's bedroom is downstairs but she was sleeping on her good ear and didn't hear a thing. It stopped just as I reached it. I waited for a while, and then returned upstairs to my bedroom. The phone began ringing again. This time, after about four rings, and nearly breaking my neck on the unlighted staircase, I made it; and I was right — it was an emergency. It was my young cousin Sister Partridge sobbing and crying hysterically.

"What is it?" I kept asking her. "Sister, what is it?"

Finally, she blurted out, "Daddy's dead! Daddy's dead!"

"What happened?" I kept asking. "Sister, how did it happen?"

But she was too upset to talk further with me. Her brother-in-law Cappy came to the phone simply to tell me that Fod had had a heart attack, "a massive coronary," earlier in the evening and that he was dead on arrival by the time Sister got him to the Ellsworth Hospital.

Cappy thought my mother and I should know, since we had been so close over the years. I thanked him and went in to wake Sid to tell her. Her only reaction was, "I'm not surprised. I've been expecting something like this ever since those awful nosebleeds started."

The nosebleeds had started the summer before. Fod had refused to do anything about them until the night of Sister's graduation from high school when he insisted on being present in the school gym. Sister's older sisters, Lovina, Cappy's wife, and Spunky, tried to make him stay in his truck but he wouldn't. He also wouldn't let them try and pack his nose. Lovina later told me, "It was awful — the spectacle he made. His nice white dress shirt, the only one he owned, was covered with blood. Finally, Spunky took him by his hand to the Ellsworth Hospital and how he hated that hospital. He kept yelling at us, 'Get me out of this goddamn place!' "

Fod had had high blood pressure for years and yet he kept right on smoking, drinking, over-eating, not exercising, sitting around his trailer watching TV and talking on his CB radio. He also had this huge wen growing on the back of his neck which he wouldn't let the doctor remove. He said when it swelled up he could tell the weather by it.

"Let's face it," Lovina said later, "he was overweight and out-of-date!"

But it hadn't always been so. In his younger years, Fod had been an exceptionally good-looking man. Tall, dark-haired, and stern looking, he had posed for a photograph in his U.S. Army uniform, a picture that still hung in Lovina's living room. Fod had been a soldier in World War II in Germany, and like many other Maine veterans of that war, he termed it "the best time of my life." He had brought back a dead Nazi's fancy sword and a pistol which he liked to show to us kids. Fod was always telling his Army stories. When I mentioned to him about my teaching black kids in Syracuse during the "race riot days" of the late 1960's and early 1970's, he told me about knowing some Negroes in the Army. One tale was about a Negro driving a truck. The Negro stopped the truck by some American troops, one of whom was Uncle Fod, who warned the Negro driver that the Krauts were just around the corner. "I turn 'round right chere!" said the Negro. Fod loved that line, and he kept repeating it. Fod's stories were always like that, too. He once told me a Maine story about asking for directions. It seems Uncle Fod, with his family, was in South Paris one time driving around trying to find his brother's house, when he stopped and asked an old man standing in a field for directions. The old man looked right at Fod and screamed, "Ma well's dry!" Fod was always having such encounters.

Fod's mother died when he was very young growing up in a poor Downeast family of five brothers and five sisters. After his mother's death, he lived in a succession of foster homes around Taunton, finally spending his teenage years with an older brother and his wife. Just before World War II, he got a job at one of Taunton's two lobster pounds, and was married to his first wife soon thereafter. He enlisted in the Army when the war broke out; and after the war he came home to a divorce from his wife. Rumor around town had it that Fod's older brother and wife had helped break up the marriage.

Throughout the war and for a few years after, regular dances were held every week at the old East Side Grange Hall in Taunton; and even though Fod didn't like to dance, he'd fix himself up nice after work and hang around the hall where he met Eller Warren, my mother's younger sister, who was also recently divorced with two little children. Fod and Eller were married in late 1946. They set up housekeeping in a little house right next door to my family's; and proceeded to have four more children. After the war, Fod had returned to his old job at the Pound, where he drove a lobster truck back and forth three times a week between Taunton and Gloucester, Massachusetts.

Fod was a very slow, but good driver. He always drove around twenty miles an hour, no matter what. He was disgusted when they raised the speed limit in Taunton to 35. At the speed he traveled, we always wondered how he drove the lobster truck three times a week back and forth to Massachusetts. In the early sixties, after a fatal accident on the Waldo-Hancock suspension bridge, whereby a car ran into the back of his lobster truck on an icy winter night, Fod was really scared to drive; and even more so after Aunt Eller was killed in a car accident in 1964. In the last years of his working life, when he was driving a truck for a construction company in Portland, Cappy, who worked for the same company then, remembers how all the men were going to take Fod to the Tammy Wynette show at the Portland Civic Center; but he went and hid in the grader, because he didn't want to drive in the Portland traffic.

Fod wasn't much of a father. Because of his foster home upbringing, he probably didn't know how to be one. He and Eller did take the kids on Sunday afternoon excursions all over Maine, especially down to Washington County on the "CC Road," which was really the "CCC Road," for Civilian Conservation Corps; and to such places as Spring River Lake and Nicatous. There would be drives and picnics down roads that aimlessly wandered. Fod would always take along a bottle of water and a box of crackers. The kids remembered how Fod and Eller would both have to get out of the car and pee from time to time by the side of the road.

Fod's life was ritualized. He'd get up very early in the morning and his rounds never varied. He'd insist that the bread be kept in the refrigerator; his chair was the rocking chair in the kitchen by the window. On Saturday nights, he and Eller would get good and drunk on beer and raise hell. During one of these sessions, when I was visiting my cousins, he decided to kick me out. "It's time you went to home!" he yelled at me, and before I could move, he kicked me in the rear end, and kept kicking me out the door. That was the only time I personally experienced Fod's violence; but his kids would often tell about his nasty temper.

In later years, when Eller had died, and Fod had moved with his youngest daughter Sister into a trailer, he'd visit Sid and me when I was home from teaching; and we'd swap stories. I liked him at such times; but Sid was always wary of him, because as the sister-in-law who lived next door all those years, she had seen and knew too much. "He's a drunk," she'd say, "and he gets awful mean."

Often I'd stop by his trailer and sometimes I'd bring some of my New York students with me. One time I had a handsome lad with me named Bo who was interested in seeing the College of the Atlantic in Bar Harbor. Bo was a senior in high school at the time; and he stood six foot three. Upon entering Fod's trailer, Bo had to duck his head; and Fod greeted him by saying, "A feller like you must play BAR-skit ball! Do ya play a lot of BAR-skit ball?"

"Not too much," Bo said. "I'm into skiing."

"Yeah? Well, you're a good-looking son-of-a-bitch, so I bet the women in them ski lodges go for your balls!"

"Well, once in a while," said Bo, who kept grinning sheepishly at me, wondering no doubt what in hell he had walked into.

Fod was sitting in his rocking chair with his cap on that had "10-4" stenciled on it and was about half way through a six pack of Narragansett. At one point, cousin Sister, who had grown up to be quite a stout girl, entered the room with a wild-acting kitten.

"Look out for that damn kitty!" said Fod. "He's half bobcat. You dangle your hand down in front of him, and he'll dig and claw ya until you're all scratched and bloody! Sister made him wild like that."

"Oh, he's just a growing tomcat," said Sister, who spent most of our visit eyeing handsome Bo.

"We're gonna have to get his balls cut off," said Fod, "so he'll stop clawing the shit out of everything."

"You get a lot of action on your CB?" asked Bo.

"Some nights," said Fod. "I like to hear 'em yelling back and forth from the boats out in the bay. Sometimes there's a funny remark. Mostly just swearing and complaining, though."

Upon our leaving, Sister, who spent most of her days watching soap operas on TV and lunching, said to me, "Jesus, An-day. That guy's a real hunk! Bring home a few more of your students like that!"

And in the car, as we drove away from the trailer park, I asked Bo what he thought of our visit.

He smiled and shook his head. "That cousin of yours was trying to rape me; but I liked Fod. Seems like he's got a few stories to tell."

"He can be very good company," I said.

And so he could, especially in later years, when he was given to reminiscing a great deal about his Taunton boyhood. I even made a tape recording of him once telling about chopping down trees in the old days.

And now he was dead. He had evidently had the attack in the living room and called out to Sister who was down the hall in her bedroom. She had come running and he was gasping for breath. Somehow, she got him out of the trailer and into her old, beat-up, red Opal. Screaming and crying all the way, while he lay gasping and dying beside her, Sister drove like a wild woman down the back road to Ellsworth as fast as the car would go through the night in the rain, her flashing lights turned on, and leaning on the horn. Hysterical by that time, she really didn't know that her father was dead when they lugged him into the hospital.

It occurred to me that I should call Fod's two stepdaughters, my cousins Lillie in Alaska and Kitty in Utah, who even though they hated him and had left home in the middle of high school because of his sexual advances and beatings, should know. Since it was earlier in both places than in Maine, I decided to call right away.

Lillie's reaction was quiet. "I guess he had it coming to him," she said. "I'm not particularly sorry. I guess I don't feel anything. There was never any love there. How is Sister bearing up?"

"Well," I said, "she's pretty upset; but she's staying at Lovina's."

"He was a negative and brutal man," she said, "and probably very frustrated and unhappy. I never really knew him. I'll call Sister tomorrow. Please let me know if there's anvthing I can do for her or the family."

"I will."

Cousin Kitty was much more bitter and angry. When I told her, she shouted over the phone, "Good! I'm glad he's dead! He was a bastard. You don't really expect me to send a sympathy card, do you?"

"No, but you might write to Sister. She's pretty broken up."

"All right; but please don't expect me to feel sorry for that man. He was an evil son-of-a-bitch. He hated me and I hated him. He slapped me all the time. I couldn't get away from him fast enough; and my memories of him are all ugly."

"I understand how you feel, Kitty; I just thought you ought to know."

"O.K., well, now I know. He's dead and gone right to hell where he belongs."

Only a few relatives and neighbors were at Fod's graveside service at Taunton's beautiful Riverview Cemetery, where I used to tend a number of the lots, and where my grandparents, father, and many of my relatives and family friends were buried. It was a dramatic summer day, muggy and stormy. With the thunderclouds gathering overhead and the wind picking up, it looked like it was about to pour at any moment.

I was glad to see that the Reverend Harvey Phillips, a modest, mild-mannered Maine minister, was officiating. He had also presided over the funerals of Aunt Eller, my father, and other members of our family; so it seemed natural and comforting to have him there. In his eulogy, Reverend Phillips mentioned how Fod had driven a lobster truck for twenty-five years, how he had even driven a truck for the Rockefellers, and how he had loved his CB radio. Just as he was saying the last prayer, there was a wild flash of lightning and a heavy crash of thunder. "Hurry up and bury him!" said Lovina, who was frightened to death of thunderstorms. And just in time it was over, and everyone made a mad dash to their cars. I did overhear Lovina, who, when she passed by the nosy Garrett neighbor women with whom our family had always feuded, say, "Well, howdy, girls! Came to make sure he was dead, right? Well, there he is. Take a good look. Satisfy your curiosity!"

A bitter, brief funeral for a man few had ever loved. A Downeast Protestant wake followed at Fod's older brother's house amidst the downpour. One of my cousins ran her car off the road into the ditch, and people were scurrying into the house between thunderclaps carrying food covered over by saran wrap and newspapers. The little house was jammed with relatives, hot and uncomfortable; but we did manage to talk a little with each other, not much about Fod, but about our lives and the prospects for the summer.

Sister, and Fod's only son Buster, got hugged and kissed a lot; and they both broke down; but everyone else, including Lovina and Spunky, Fod's two older daughters, kept a poker-faced, dry-eyed vigil. All Lovina said to me, at one point, was, "All Daddy thought he could ever do was drive a truck; and I guess he was right."

THE SOAP OPERA

SITTING AT THE KITCHEN TABLE having coffee at my cousin Lovina's house in Jefferson one Saturday morning, I was trying to find out from her about her younger brother, Buster, to see how he was getting along.

"That's a very sore subject," she said. "Anybody who has had anything to do with him has a bad memory."

Lovina's a good-looking, hard-working Maine housewife in her mid-thirties, married to her truck driver husband, Cappy, and the mother of two children. Lovina's got a good head on her shoulders, and to help make ends meet, she does part-time work at the nearby Jefferson Grocery and in the summers she rakes blueberries. Growing up in Taunton Ferry down the road from me, she moved to Jefferson when she married Cappy. Brother Buster, however, is not one of her favorite topics, so I had to be careful in what I said.

"Is Buster working in Portland now?" I asked.

"Yes, and I heard he's planning on getting married again."

"Really? Do you know to whom?"

"Probably someone he met in AA. That's his social life these days."

"He hasn't had a drink in over two years now, isn't it?"

"I don't know, and to be honest, An-day, I don't care. I've lost count. It's just a relief to me that he's moved out of the area. He burned us so bad for so long, I've just tried to put him out of my mind and out of my life."

But I persisted. "He was good at Sister's wedding," I said.

"Yes, that's true; he was. Miracles do happen, I guess, but I've got to give him more time to see if he's really changed. God, the last time he was here, when he was drinking, you know what he did?"

"Nope."

"He got up in the night and pissed in the toaster! You should have smelled my kitchen the next morning!"

"He was always doing something like that."

"He sure was and it's not funny! He owes everyone in this family, including you, I bet, a lot of money, money we couldn't afford."

"Yes, that's true. He's borrowed from me over the years."

"Borrowed? You'll never see your money again. He got into so many damn scrapes and Daddy and Mama always took up for him, always got him off. After they both died, he started in depending upon us, but it didn't work, and I hope by this point he knows he's got to grow up and make a living on his own."

"But, of course, Lovina, he's an alcoholic and so he's sick. He can't help it."

"I know. That's why it was a good first step when he went to AA in Bangor. They have helped him; that's for sure."

"What's he doing in Portland?"

"Operating a back hoe, or something. He's working for a construction company."

"Remember that time he stole the bulldozer that weekend and drove out to one of the lakes around here and asked some camp-owners if there was anything they wanted dug up?"

"Yes, that's how he lost that job. That's what he always kept doing. Getting drunk and stealing and getting into trouble. And then expecting his family to come to his rescue."

"He was always so stupid about his crimes, like the time he set off the fire alarm at the court house in Ellsworth. He just stood there until the police came and arrested him."

"That was a federal offense, ya know."

"Yes, I know. My favorite caper of Buster's was that heist of all those musical instruments from the music store in Ellsworth. Remember how the Taunton Police caught Buster and his gang, all trying to have a jam session in your living room?"

"Yes, and not a one of 'em could even play a note! That must have been quite a concert!"

"Whatever happened to the other gang members?"

"Howie works over to Bucksport with his older brother selling woodstoves; and as far as I know, Gus Stratton and Wilbur Carter are still bumming around."

"I'll never forget the night, when I was just home for Christmas vacation in 1976, and my article on worm-digging had just appeared in the New York *Times*, when Buster and Wilbur showed up, drunk out of their minds, with a wrinkled copy of my article. They wanted me to write up about their big bear hunt and print it in the *Times.* It took us quite a while to convince them that unless their bear hunt was a very unusual one, the New York *Times* wouldn't be interested."

"I didn't know about that incident, but I'm only surprised that anyone as illiterate as Buster would even know that the New York *Times* existed."

"Whatever happened to his wife and kids?"

"You mean The Carnival Queen? I don't really know. Last I heard they had moved further Downeast to Machias or some place."

"Buster worked with her in the carnival, didn't he?"

"Yes, her whole family would travel around with the carnival in the summertime, and then be on welfare the rest of the year."

"She was something, wasn't she?"

"What other type of woman would team up with someone like Buster?"

"Were any of those kids his?"

"He claimed one of 'em."

"One night when I was home for another of my Christmas vacations, I took a little gift up to them in that old beat-up trailer they used to live in behind the box factory at the Junction. Remember that?"

"Sure. That was a real den of sin."

"What got me was the trailer was upended. They had it sort of propped up on one side and everything was at an angle inside, like a sinking ship."

"And I bet the inhabitants didn't even notice! All they did was drink and party all the time; and they were on welfare."

"That night, they must have been with their carnival cronies, for they looked like a hard crowd. They were getting hooched on beer and cheap wine and they seemed to be playing some kind of card game while the kids were watching TV. I sat with them for a while and had a beer, but the conversation wasn't exactly scintillating. Buster was loaded to the gills and trying to tell me some plan of his about starting his own construction company."

"With the bulldozer he stole, no doubt! God, yes, pipe dreams and plans, and so little reality. He was never playing with a full deck those years. He'd have one of his little capers and we'd end up paying his bills, or bailing him out."

"But how could he help it, Lovina, with that awful upbringing he had?"

"That's no excuse! We all had the same upbringing; and I'm living a decent, hard-working life. So are the rest of the kids, except Buster."

"But he was the only boy; and both Uncle Fod and Aunt Eller doted on him and made so much out of him. They spoiled him. I remember one time I was staying down at your house, and we took turns watching through the register from upstairs an awful row downstairs between Fod and Eller. They were screaming at each other and alternately pulling Buster, who must have been only about ten or so, back and forth between them."

"They were both alcoholics, too."

"I know; but scenes like that have certainly stayed with me; and must have had a much greater impact on Buster. You girls often escaped by running down the road to our house."

"Yes, that's true, but we girls didn't escape Fod when he was drunk and wanted to make some advances."

"Is that why Lil and Kitty left home so soon?"

"You know it is!"

"He never attacked you, did he?"

"He tried once, but I set him straight right off and he never bothered me again."

"I remember as a kid one night I was staying down and we were all sleeping in the same bed upstairs, when, all of a sudden, Aunt Eller bangs open the door, and she's standing there illuminated from behind by the hall light stark naked with a beer bottle in her hand! It scared us so, that the bed collapsed! Remember?"

Lovina laughed. "Sure. Fod came after her with a German pistol that he had taken off the dead body of a German soldier during the war. He chased her downstairs with it. And we ran to the window overlooking the backyard and watched him chasing her with the gun around the yard in the night with mama's chickens racing to get out of the way. He kept yelling he was going to kill her. She had been taunting him that night about his being a big war hero with his Nazi sword and pistol that he kept in his bedroom closet. She often started their fights."

"Yes, I remember her line that she kept repeating. She said, 'If you're a goddamn war hero, then I'm the fucking Maine Dairy Queen!' She said that because at the time she was driving the milk truck."

"It is true that Mama'd often start the fights. She was a mean drunk and she'd get him going till he was in a rage. That night I really thought he was going to kill her, but, of course, the gun wasn't loaded."

"Where was Buster that night?" I asked. "I don't remember him being there."

"I don't either."

"Maybe he was hiding."

"You want some more coffee?"

"Well, maybe a half a cup."

Lovina poured me some more, while I continued reminiscing.

"Later, after Fod had died, and Buster had lost his license for a series of drunk driving accidents, he called me up late one night, after midnight, and begged me to come up to the trailer park and see him. It was pouring rain, but I went. I remember sitting there while he told me about the great singing career he was planning for himself. He had written this song, which was about the rain. An appropriate number, you see; but he would start playing and he couldn't get the guitar tuned right, so he kept starting and stopping. I thought he'd never get beyond the first line. It was a very sad and mournful wail that came out of him, too. After he finished the song, and I told him what I thought, he hit me up for twenty-five dollars."

"Yeah, what'd I tell ya."

"Do you know if he's still playing his guitar?"

"Yes, I heard he's now in a band and they play at nights in a Portland laundromat. When I heard that, I said he ought to call his band The Soap Opera!"

CHECKING IN WITH THE HARBOR MASTER

I WAS HAVING A SUNDAY AFTERNOON DINNER with my mother Sid and my older brother Bobber when I happened to mention that I would probably drop by and see Fat on my way back to Orono and the start of another schoolteaching week. Ever since he lost the use of his legs, and was confined to a walker and a kitchen rocking chair, Fat was probably awfully lonely and depressed. Once on the go all of his life, he never got out at all now unless someone took him. But my mother objected to my visits, as she did about anything having to do with Fat Moon.

"Why do you want to bother seeing that wicked old man? He's so awful."

"I feel sorry for him, and I am fascinated by him."

"Fascinated? You're crazy! He never did anything for anyone else, and certainly nothing for you."

"He brought me some mackerel a few times."

"And that was when he was going senile."

"Why are you so against him? I've never understood that."

"Oh, I don't know," she said. "I guess it's all his foolish talk. He never did any work, but he always got the credit for it."

"He used to go lobstering, didn't he?"

"Yeah," said Bobber, "I used to go with him and Dad."

"What was that like?"

"They used to tie me on the front of the boat. That's probably why today I'm still wary of boats out on the ocean. Used to scare the hell out of me when we got out beyond the bay and there was a normal heavy sea of two or three foot waves. Since I was tied onto the front of the boat, and a little kid, I'd be looking first down into the ocean and then up at the sky. It was goddamn scary! But now, of course, I realize that the lobster boat was very seaworthy."

"Where did Fat have his traps?"

"All over the place, but mostly he had one string of 'em along the East Taunton shore and then the other side of the bay over by West Hamlin. So, when he'd go out, he'd haul his traps on this side first and then put out his fish line, then haul his traps over on the Hamlin side. He'd basically just keep goin' around in circles."

"Did you help him?"

"Yeah, one of my jobs was helping to bait the fish line. You know those tubs of fish lines they used to have?"

"I guess so."

"Well, there would be several hundred feet of cord line. It has a certain lay to it, ya know, so it has to be laid in the tub just one way. Well, you'd throw it overboard, and as each hook came up — there were a couple of hundred hooks on a line — you'd bait it. Later, when we came back from hauling the Hamlin side traps, they'd pull the fish line and there would be just the heads of some of the fish stuck on the hooks where the dogfish had gotten to 'em. The sight of that used to make me even more alarmed."

"How did that work with the fish line? Did they attach them to the lobster buoys?"

"No, they dropped an anchor with one of their buoys and attached the line with their flag on it, so no one else would pull it. Later, it was another of my jobs to stretch out the used fish lines and re-tub them."

"Those were the mackerel?"

"Yeah, mostly. Fat used to peddle them around town, along with his lobsters, and he used to dry fish, too."

"Yes, I remember the dry fish. One time he ripped off a piece for me to eat and it was full of maggots."

"He probably made you eat it anyway, didn't he?"

"Yes. He said it wasn't any good without maggots. Dad was there and they were eating it, and I felt I better not look like a sissy. Fat used to dry the fish out in back of his house all over the place. That's probably how the maggots got into it."

"It just got rotten," Bobber said.

"Did he sell his lobsters to one of the local pounds?" I asked.

"I don't know. I guess so. I can't remember. All the men in those days kept their own lobsters in lobster cars tied off in the cove. You know, down here in the cove where he kept his boat in the wintertime."

"Yes. We used to play down there all the time."

"Sure. Each fisherman in those days had his own little anchorage and one of the two guys would share their own cove. They had their little on-shore work area where they stored their traps, barrels, and equipment. Made great playhouses for the younger generation."

"Did Fat ever get mad at you?"

"He got outraged if anyone got near his stuff. But all the men did, since that was how they made their living."

"Women liked Fat, didn't they?"

"Yes!" interrupted Sid. "Since he used to take 'em to the dances all the time and make all that foolish talk; but I always thought he was repulsive."

"But he must have had something," I said.

"He looks just like a bulldog," she said. "Remember that one he had? When he was with that dog, it was hard to tell 'em apart. And he'd make such fools out of the summer people. They all thought he was so great; then he'd be fleecing them for all he could."

"But wasn't that the standard practice along the whole coast?"

"Of course. Everyone stole a little bit. It was more or less accepted, but Fat Moon overdid it!"

"But he brought up Dad. I remember always going to visit Fat every Sunday afternoon with Dad."

"Sure, but even your father got sick of him after he found out about all the stealing."

"You mean more than the usual with the summer people?"

"Yes. You know all those hundreds of tools he's got up there? Where do you think he got them all? He had one of everything. If you ever needed anything, you could go up to Fat's."

"That's right," Bobber said. "He got caught when he got older, I remember."

"Yes," said Sid. "It was out west, when he and Emma were on one of their trips. They had to bail him out of jail for his shoplifting. He was actually a kleptomaniac. He even built houses for the summer people with stolen lumber. Then he charged them double, and played up to 'em down on the dock; and they'd take pictures of him as the Old Maine Salt and think he was wonderful."

"Well, in a way, he was," I said. "I remember how when he was the Harbor Master, he'd sit down there on the dock or in the boathouse all day and welcome the tourists to God's Country!"

"And pocket a charge on every boat that needed a mooring," said Bobber.

"Yes, and that's what I find so sickening about him," said Sid.

"But you'd go on the picnics and boat trips out in the bay and take us kids," I said.

"Well, of course, I went along with your father. But that doesn't mean I ever enjoyed it."

"I'm going up to see him anyway," I said.

"Suit yourself."

And so I did.

The place hadn't changed since I was a kid. The familiar old clamshell driveway still encircled the house, which had been Fat's grandfather's, perched halfway up a hill overlooking Frenchman's Bay with a panoramic view of the Mount Desert Hills. It was an old sea captain's house. Fat was 88 and his common-law wife Emma was 92. For over thirty years they had lived together. Fat had been married to my late paternal grandmother even when Emma came to live with them; but my grandmother had been dead for twenty-five years.

The only thing that was different was that Fat's car, his truck, and his boats were all gone. His backyard was more picked up, but inside there were the same glaring fluorescent lights in the kitchen, the same furniture, the same smell. And there was Fat in his chair with the aluminum walker in front of him with dozens of his tools hooked to it.

"Come on in! Come on in!" he said in his familiar gruff voice.

"Hi, Fat. Remember me?" I asked, entering the kitchen.

"Well, for god's sake, yes. Emma! Emma!" he hollared.

"If she's lying down, you don't need to bother her."

"No. I want her to bring you something that was your father's."

"What is it?"

"A set of deer horns. Don't you want 'em?"

"Sure, I guess so. One of his bucks?"

"Yeah. He got three or four that year, like he always did. Your father was a goddamn good hunter."

"I know."

Emma appeared in the doorway, looking as ladylike and as skinny as she ever did. She was such a handsome gentlewoman and Fat was such a scruffy old harbor master that they made quite the odd couple, sort of like Venus and Vulcan.

"Hi, Emma."

"Well, hello."

"Go git them horns for him!"

"All right." She disappeared into one of the back rooms.

Fat and I sat facing each other. He was definitely failing, but he was also still as tough as tripe, just the way I had always known him. The skin below his eyes was sagging so that there were big red splotches under his eyes. His skin over-all was more wrinkled than ever and he did look like a bull dog. He still had a steel gray crewcut. His shirt was open so that one could see his undershirt straining to contain the rolls of fat. While his real name was Arthur, it was easy to see how he came by his nickname. Beside him was a pot to pee in, and knowing Fat, if he had to, he would, right there in front of everyone. That was part of his animal charm.

"She is re-MACK-able, ain't she?" he asked, or rather stated.

"She certainly is. I don't see how she does it."

"Christ, she's re-MACK-able!" he said again with renewed emphasis.

To get along with Fat, you had to trade insults with him, and so I said, "I don't know how she stands it to take care of you."

"I know it! Christ, I'm goddamn lucky. Otherwise, I'd be in the goddamn nursing home."

"You'd really be cussing then, wouldn't ya?"

"I guess probably! Those places are no damn good. That's where a man has to go when no one gives a damn, when there's no hope left. They just like to make money off unfortunate old folks with no good families. It's a rotten business, I don't care what ya say."

"I agree with you."

"Yeah, but by Jesus, you'd put me in there, right along with the whole lot of ya who don't even bother to stop by and see me!"

"What about Uncle Wallace? Doesn't he come down often?"

"Not since I drove him off!"

"What did you do that for?"

"He tried to tell me the land beyond this house, between this house and his, *is his*! I guess I set him straight, and he ain't been back since."

At this point, Emma returned with the horns. She gave them to me.

"That's a beautiful set," I said. "Thank you."

"Well, they belong at your father's house, not anywhere else, so I want you to have 'em."

Emma sat down beside me and we both faced Fat.

"Why did both you and Dad not like Uncle Wallace?" I asked.

"He's no damn good!"

"What do you mean?"

"He was lazy and wouldn't do any work! When your father Frank would be out chopping wood, Wallace would be in here taking a nap! One time Frank almost killed him, and it would have been a good thing if he had!"

"Well, I could never figure out why they never spoke to each other while I was growing up."

"That's why."

"I've always wanted to know, Fat — was that fast cabin cruiser of yours that we used to go on picnics in — was that boat used for rum-running during Prohibition?"

"Damn right it was! Could outrun anything the Coast Guard had."

"Were you a rum-runner?"

"If you had a boat like that, you'd have been damn foolish if you weren't. We had a right to get in on some of the money and fun up here in Maine, too, ya know."

I changed the subject. "Since Dr. Bounty died, who's been taking you shopping every week, Boyd and Carrie?"

"No! They did for a while, but then they got high class and moved down to Bay Harbor. With all their new friends and social life, they can't be bothered now."

"What about Billy Brown?"

"He was gonna come by today and take us on a ride to see the leaves, but he's got to take his wife to the hospital. I think she's got cancer of the spine."

"Really? That's terrible."

"Well, she's had everything else. Billy's always having to look after her and take her to one damn doctor after another. He said he'd try to take us to see the leaves next weekend, but now's the time. Won't be any sense going next week. The colors won't be as bright as they are today."

"Oh, I think they'll still be quite spectacular."

"No, they won't!"

All this time that we talked, Emma said nothing. She just sat there. I asked her a few questions, but she only gave me mostly one-syllable answers. At one point, she got up to say she was going down cellar to get some Crisco.

"I'll get it for you, Emma," I said. "Where do you keep it?"

"Right down at the bottom of the cellar stairs on the shelves to your left."

I hadn't been down in their cellar for years, and I was astounded when I saw all the stuff they had down there. Cases of everything: canned milk, sardines, vinegar, all kinds of canned goods, and several boxes of cans of Crisco.

"My God," I said upon returning to the kitchen, "you've got enough food down there to feed the whole town for five years! Is this some kind of designated fallout shelter or something?"

"Ya never know when you'll be snowed in by a blizzard," said

Fat. "And since ya can't depend on anyone to drive ya to the store, it's best we have plenty of supplies right here."

"You don't have to go to the store for years."

"Probably not, but, by Jesus! I'd like to get out of this kitchen once in a while!"

"Well, I can't take ya out today, but maybe I will sometime."

"Yeah, sometime! You're just like the rest of 'em. You'd think the goddamn government would have some kind of service; but look at these damn selectmen we've got running this town!"

"Did you ever run for selectman, Fat?"

"No, I'm a big enough crook as it is!"

"Well, then, what are you complaining about? At least you're not in the hospital in that oxygen tent like you were last spring, with all of those tubes and wires running in and out of you."

"I ripped that tent right off! That's what saved me! Ripped all that stuff right off!"

"You didn't look like you were in much of a ripping condition when I visited you."

"I was trying to sleep when you were there bothering me!"

"Well, I won't bother you any more today. I've got to get back to Orono before nightfall. You take care of yourself, and you, too, Emma. Thanks again for the deer horns."

"You're welcome," said Emma. "Drive carefully."

"I will. Goodbye, Fat."

"Goodbye! Goodbye!" he hollared in his gruff voice.

When I got back to Orono, I phoned Sid, and she asked, "Did you stop and see Fat?"

"Yes."

"Was he full of his usual foolish talk and swearing?"

"Yes, but I sort of enjoy his rage."

"Outrage, you mean," she said. "He loves hating the world. That's what keeps him going."

"Well, whatever it is, I still find him fascinating."

"Yes, you would," she said. "You've always gotten along with the weirdest people."

THE NOISE THAT CLOUDS MAKE

EVERY TIME THERE'S A THUNDERSTORM in our neighborhood, if it starts before midnight, you can be sure Hanky and Bibben Ray, our next door neighbors for the past thirty years, will be sitting in our kitchen or living room until the last thunderclap has clapped. If it's past midnight, and they're in bed, they'll get out of bed, get dressed, and go out in the driveway and sit in their Chevette for the duration. If they happen to see a light on at our house, then they'll drive up and come inside. They've been doing this ever since they moved into the neighborhood from the old Consolidated Lobster Pound where they used to live.

Bibben's a big-boned, tall woman who wears high-heeled shoes, her hair piled high on her head, and who has a great penchant for jewelry. She's got a ring on nearly every finger and is always decked out in all manner of clanky bracelets, dangling earrings, and sparkling necklaces, even when she's doing a wash for one of the summer people. In contrast, her husband Hanky is a small, bespectacled man who always sports a set of suspenders and a nondescript hat. He's very proud of his lifelong, unwavering, and adamant support of Maine Republicans and conservative causes. Hanky doesn't want anything ever to change and he votes accordingly. Both Bibben and Hanky are hypochondriacs and drive to the Bar Harbor Hospital every week for their regular checkups. They claim to have had every ailment that has come down the pike. When Betty Ford and Happy

Rockefeller had their well-publicized mastectomies, it wasn't long before Bibben had one, too.

One night last summer, I had just gotten home for my vacation, when it started storming and thundering to beat the band; and in drove the Rays. They rushed in the house between cloudbursts, and Bibben had a cast on her left arm.

Once settled in our living room, my mother Sid said, "Bibben, I hope you've learned your lesson, but you probably haven't."

"I guess probably," said Bibben. "What worries me is if I can play twenty-one cards tonight at Beano."

"It'll probably be fun watching ya try," my mother said, "but I would think you'd want to rest up after such a bad fall."

"What happened?" I asked. "I came in late, remember?"

"Oh, Bibben had on her spike heels up to the grammar school, and she caught one in a rubber mat, and took a spill," said Sid.

"Trying to catch herself, she broke her arm," said Hanky. "Jesus!"

"Well, ya know," said Bibben, "Lydia busted her arm last winter and she still played the same number she always did. Didn't affect her any and it won't me."

"That's the spirit, Bibben!" I said. "Remember, you're a pro. Don't give up. Play *forty* cards! Go for it!"

"Quiet, An-day," said Sid.

Bibben chuckled, as she did every time I said anything to her. She was also in the habit, ever since my childhood, of taking my face between her hands and kissing me full on the lips, but, with her broken arm, she didn't attempt to kiss me this time.

"I used to play forty cards," she said, "and MaryAnn Page still does."

"What about you, Hanky; how many do you play?"

Before he could answer, Bibben said, "Oh, he only plays a dozen. He'd rather just smoke and talk. He doesn't take his beano as serious as I do."

"What I don't understand," said Sid, "is how you can play all those cards and run the concession stand at the same time."

"Well, we always go up early Saturday afternoon and get set up. Hanky's got his own key to the school, since he's the janitor. Once we get it all set up, it's easy enough to keep going. People usually help me out when I have a rush at one of the breaks."

"Do you still sell those delicious crabmeat sandwiches?" I asked. "That's what I remember from beano."

"We do, but I don't make 'em any more; and hardly anyone buys them since that Alberta Martin has been makin' 'em."

"Why not?"

"Well, she's such a big fat slob — ya know, the one who lives in the trailer up near the North Taunton Bait Shop. She's got a big butt on her that sticks out like I don't know what. She always wears slacks and sweaters to beano. She just ain't neat, so people won't eat her stuff."

At this point, there was a brilliant flash followed by a louder than usual thunderclap.

"Godfrey mighty! How I hate that awful noise those big black clouds make! They've always scared me half to death!" said Bibben.

"Jesus!" Hanky said.

"Have you ever been hit?" I asked.

"No, but I still hate it; and I've seen the damage that's been done."

"This house has been hit three times," I said, "once during my lifetime."

"The last time it blew up our television set," my mother said, "and nearly killed me."

"I was playing monopoly," I said, "at the kitchen table with Cousin Lillie and my friend Russell Barclay. Russell was sort of tipped back in his chair and when the lightning hit the TV and blew out all the lights, he went right over backwards onto the floor."

"After it blew up the TV," Sid said, "that nice GE console we had, it crossed the room and hit a nail on the wall right above my head; ripped the wallpaper right off the wall!"

"Jesus!" said Hanky.

"Yes, I remember that time now," said Bibben. "It split a tree right down the middle down in the backfield, and it also tore a clapboard off your house where it entered, didn't it?"

"Yes, and we never replaced it," said Sid.

"Well, I hope tonight isn't the fourth time we get hit," said Hanky, "but Christ, it's awful sharp."

"Tell me more about beano games in the old days," I said. "Where did you play before the new school was built?"

"Up at the old Grange Hall on the East Side, remember, Sid?" asked Bibben.

"Yes, we used to play just for things, not money. I won a picnic basket once. And those two little gray bedroom lamps upstairs in the front room. I got a dish strainer one time and some sugar and canned stuff."

"I remember working the floor for those games," said Hanky, "and it used to be awful trying to figure out how many cans of milk we'd have for a two dollar game."

"One time when I went up to the grammar school," I said, "I

remember this fight that broke out between two ladies over an electric blanket. They both claimed they had yelled beano first."

"I won five times in one night," said Bibben.

"Everybody went then because everybody could afford it," said Sid.

"How much did it cost?" I asked.

"You could play four cards for a dollar," said Hanky. "Extra cards were ten cents and we usually played six or eight. The only trouble with the old East Side Grange Hall was the outdoor toilets."

"Your Uncle Gene Crowley would only play two cards ever," said Bibben, "but he was the luckiest thing."

"When Gene won," said Sid, "instead of yelling out 'Beano!' like you're supposed to, he'd yell, 'Hold everything!' He was hilarious when he'd win because he'd get so excited."

"Even in the old days, at the Catholic Church they'd always play for money."

"Where else did you play?" I asked.

"We used to go to the West Hamlin Grange Hall or down to Town Hill on Mount Desert," said Bibben.

"We also just had sandwiches and coffee then," said Sid.

"Now it's all changed," said Hanky.

"How so?" I asked.

"They play different types of games now," said Bibben. "They play two Early Bird games at half-past-six. They had forty-two dollars on the first Early Bird last week. It's fifty cents a card for an Early Bird. Then, they have these Cover-All games, which is five cents a card for ten games."

"Does that mean you win when you cover the whole card?"

"Yeah, that's right. They also have Punch-Outs. Usually two of 'em and you use four paper cards, which are thrown away afterwards, and you use an ink stamper instead of chips 'n beans."

"There are sixteen games in all played on a Saturday night up at the Grammar School," said Hanky.

"Do you still play other nights besides Saturday?"

"Oh, sure. If it's good weather, and sometimes even if it ain't, you can go to Steuben, Trenton, or Verona Island on Monday; Tuesday at Hamlin; Gouldsboro on Wednesday; Thursday at the Catholic Church in Ellsworth, the VFW Hall on Friday, or you could also go up to Bangor or down to Cherryfield. And on Sundays, sometimes, we go up to Indian Island. There are a lot of people who never miss a game."

"Do you win very much?"

"Well, Madeline Guptil, who goes with us all the time, got $247 at Verona Island last week and I got twenty-two dollars. Three Thursday nights ago, I won $200 at the Catholic Church on a number game. And last Friday night, we went up to Bangor and I got twenty-five dollars. So, yes, you do win."

"You've always been lucky at beano, Bibben," said Sid.

"Two weeks ago, we didn't go any place," said Bibben.

"Why?" I asked.

"Well, it was on a Monday night. In the middle of the evening, Hanky started shaking and got hot. Madeline came right over and she said it was a kidney infection."

"How did Madeline know that?" I asked.

"Oh, Madeline has worked as a nurse's aide, ya know," said Bibben. "Anyway, we took Hanky down to the Bar Harbor hospital."

"I take it you fully recovered," I said.

"Jesus, yes!" said Hanky. "Just old age, just old age."

"Ya know, while we're talking about beano, we're having some trouble up at the grammar school," Bibben said.

"How so?"

"One of the teachers, who just moved in here from New York, and thinks she knows it all, wants 'a more careful accounting' of the funds! She's questioning my honesty, as far as I'm concerned," Hanky said.

"What do the teachers have to do with it, anyhow?"

"When they were first set up, it was agreed that the money would all go to the PTA and the school for special equipment that the teachers need and want. Now, for twenty-five years, by Jesus, I've taken care of the money, and no one has ever questioned my honesty," said Hanky.

"This teacher thinks we should be making more money," said Bibben, "when she doesn't know what she's talking about."

"There's no room for any hanky-panky, is there then?" I asked.

They all laughed at my pun. "You devil," said Bibben.

"Christ, every penny is accounted for," said Hanky. "The whole thing is strictly controlled by the State Police. You can't save seats any more and it's getting very expensive. Now we have to pay fifteen dollars for a caller and fifteen dollars for the janitor, which is me. We do get a good crowd, over a hundred usually, and so we keep around $150 on hand at all times. The beano game, we figured, since the 1950's has given the PTA, after expenses were met, over fifty thousand dollars for their kitty! And now, they're questioning our operation!"

"Hanky, I'm sure you will be able to keep that job as long as you want it," I said. "I doubt very seriously if any New York teacher would have that much say."

"Well, I might just not want it, if they keep it up," he said.

The thunderstorm finally abated and the rain let up enough so that the Rays could return home.

"You be sure," I said to Sid, on my way to finish my unpacking, "to let me know whether Bibben was able to play her twenty-one cards or not. I'll be dying to know!"

THE PERILS OF ROXANNE, THE STATE GIRL

EVERY SO OFTEN, I enjoy stopping by Cameron Smart's Finest Kind Bait Company Shop, which used to be the old Red-and-White Store in the middle of Taunton Corner across from the village green and about three miles "uptown" from where I live on the Taunton Peninsula. Cam, his wife Maxine, and I always have fun swapping stories and catching up with each other. Cam's been in the worm dealing business for about twelve years now. About seventy men dig for him and sell their bloodworms and sandworms to him, which he, Maxine, and some of the diggers' wives then package live to be shipped daily from the Bangor Airport to Boston and New York where they are sold up and down the East Coast as bait for sports fishermen. The worming season lasts from March to November (it gets a bit chilly down on the clamflats in the wintertime) and to supplement their income, Cam and Maxine operate the Finest Kind Gas Station and Drug Store, which employs about two other people part-time, pumping gas, fixing sandwiches, and manning the counter. This accounts for the seemingly strange juxtaposition on the main floor of the bait company shop of worms and seaweed with cans of oil, boxes of dry gas, and other store supplies.

Cam is a short, handsome, ruggedly-built man with curly blonde hair and bright blue eyes. He is usually in very good humor, since he enjoys telling me his yarns and about some of his business deals; but this one night a couple of weeks ago, he was rather downhearted for him and a mite perplexed over some of the crazy shenanigans some of his diggers had recently gotten themselves into.

"Do you know Tracy J?" Cam asked me.

"I don't think so," I said.

"Well, goddamn it. It's the damndest thing. He's this fellow named Tracy J. Clement. He digs for me, and he goes buggin' with this young kid, Chubby Perry, who digs for Billy Ouelette. Now Ouelette wasn't buying any worms for quite a time, so Chubby puts his worms in what they call a worm car, which is like a wooden crate. The sides are made out of nylon screen. You can't use metal because metal kills the worms. The car floats in the ocean water where the dug worms stay good and fresh."

"Of course," continued Cam, "you get the least little tear in the car and the worms escape. Well, anyway, Chubby's worm car got cut, and 30,000 worms escaped, or so he claimed. It was probably more like five thousand, but Chubby wanted to make his story sound good."

"Who's counting, anyway?"

"Yeah, that's right — who's counting! Anyway, Freddy Foss was summoned for cutting the car, which evidently he did, so Freddy got madder than hell because he got caught. Come to find out the reason he cut it was because all my diggers was digging, and he thought the worm car belonged to Tracy. It was a case of, hell, if I can't dig, I don't want you to."

"Now, Freddy Foss's woman, Jesus — God created her ugly and then kicked her in the face. The Fosses had this state child, Roxanne, a teenager about fifteen, living with them. She helps tide them over the winter months, ya see, with that income from the State of Maine."

"Cam, how cynical of you to say that."

"Well, by Jesus, it's true, ain't it? The situation with these state kids is always a scandal.

"To continue with my story, now the coastal warden summons Freddy Foss and he has to figure a way to get out of this one. Ya know, these Marine Resource Wardens, or whatever they call 'em, can search without a warrant."

"Really?"

"Shit, yes. They're second only to the IRS or the CIA."

"Back to the story."

"O.K. So you know what that Freddy Foss goes and does?"

"No."

"You know Clayton Haynesworth?"

"Sure, old Clayton."

"Christ, he's about three days older than Moses, ya know, and he rides with Freddy Foss; but Clayton don't want to dig worms with Freddy any more. This whole business, ya understand, could cost Freddy all of twenty dollars. It's a real serious offense, cutting somebody's worm car, don't ya know?

"Anyway, Freddy gets the state child, Roxanne, to admit *she* cut the car and the reason was she thought it was old Clayton's and the reason she committed such an act was because old Clayton was putting it to her, without her consent, and she didn't like being constantly molested on the mudflats. So now he was getting blackmailed from both sides. He needed a character witness, ya see, so he went to the people he digs for and told 'em he needed a character witness and they told him they'd provide him one if he dug only for them. But he didn't want to dig for 'em anymore; he wanted to dig for me. So, Clayton, who probably did pat Roxanne on the ass and feel her tits, but nothing else, wanted to try and see if these young fellers, all wormdiggers that he knew, would go down one night and gang bang Roxanne so they could all say they had her, that she was a goddamn slut, and he'd get off."

"This is terrible, Cam."

"Christ, you know as well as I do, the quality of some of the people who live and work around here. Look at Mary the Indian's daughter, Sheena! She'll dig for a fifth any time. Many diggers get paid in beer instead of money."

"Back to the story."

"Now, they were lining up the whole matter to go to court, and suddenly Billy Ouelette got really pissed off at Tracy J, because their disability checks are about the same and Billy discovered that Tracy was making more money than he was, so Tracy had to be cheating on his digging. And, of course, Chubby Perry, the kid whose car got cut in the first place, digs for Ouelette anyhow."

"So what happened? How did it all come out?"

"Chubby dropped the charges! And everything cooled right down. Once he did that, the rape charge was dropped, too. Ya know, we get these little flare-ups going every now and then amongst the dealers and diggers. It's in the blood, I guess, but this case had me worried there for a while. I thought we'd be back to slashing each other's tires again, or worse."

"What about the state girl, Roxanne? Whatever happened to her?"

"Christ, I just heard she was going to get married to Chubby Perry!"

THE MAINE NIGGER ON STAGE

EVERYONE TALKS ABOUT GARLAND COFFIN, but no one ever does anything about him.

He's really quite intelligent, you know.

But you have to admit he looks like an idiot.

The way he's always sort of hunched over, the way he squints at you through those heavy, black-rimmed glasses that are always almost falling off his face, the way he grins at you when you talk to him.

What gets me is the way he works in the dark.

In the summertime, he mows cemetery lots at night by the light of his car headlights. It's eerie to see him doing that.

One night the Taunton police reported that all was quiet except that Garland was up on his roof shingling by lantern light.

And another night they noticed he was banking his house by flashlight.

Last July, some of us were down to Olga Zumbrowski's new little summer shack on the cove and the black flies were as thick as anything, when someone noticed that Garland was out mowing the lawn in the dark with no shirt on. Olga kept calling to him out the window and telling him it was time to quit. It was nine or ten o'clock then, and he must have been covered with bites, even if he had doused himself with bug repellant.

Some people say Garland is Olga's nigger.

He's everyone's nigger. That's how he makes his living.

He's quite a worker. Just like his parents were. Garland will tackle any odd job, no matter how odd or dirty.

In school, however, Garland got all A's; but they still used to make fun of him because of his queer loner ways.

He was a strong kid. In grammar school, he used to pick up a girl he fancied and swing her around the playground as fast and as hard as he could. Helen Springer was one of the girls and she says, "I thought I was going to be thrown like a missile over the outhouse."

One time on the Ellsworth schoolbus, when Garland was in high school, on a dare, a pretty cheerleader kissed him right on the lips, to the great amusement of her classmates.

Still, there were others who hardly noticed him. "He was just there," they say.

They also say that Garland's the result of "poor seed," since his parents, Elias and Evie Coffin, didn't have him until after they had been married for twenty years and were into their forties.

The midwife was shocked when she heard that Evie Coffin was going to have a baby.

Elias and Evie, like Elias' parents before him, used to deliver fresh water in wooden crates with four, four-gallon bottles in them down on Taunton Point to the summer people who didn't want to drink the town water that was pumped out of an old mine.

The Coffins used a windmill to pump the water out of their well. They never had electricity on their farm. Elias was little, hunched-over, and serious-looking, just like Garland, while Evie was big, tall, and raw-boned. They worked hard all the time.

Except they were great grange-goers. They drove all over the state in that funny-looking homemade truck of theirs.

It was really a Model-T Ford converted with a large wooden addition with windows stuck on the back. Margie Hanson, the cheerleader who kissed Garland, used to claim that it was the first mobile home on wheels in America.

It looked like something the Okies would have traveled in during Depression days. You'd never think it would go ten feet, but, by God, the Coffins took it to Florida and back several times, and once they even went to California in it. They always repaired it themselves.

It was on one of their grange excursions upcountry that Garland met Julie.

Everyone was shocked when they got married, especially Elias and Evie. They did everything they could to prevent it, but they couldn't. The wedding was pretty nice, except when Julie threw her bouquet, Garland caught it! And then later, after the marriage, when Julie wanted to move out of the house, away from Garland's parents, the parents had a fit. They didn't want to lose their boy.

That's when Garland and Julie bought the old Gordon Hayes place just down the road from his parents.

And not long after that their son Timmy was born.

He's a real bright boy, everybody says.

But then, Julie started having all those awful car accidents.

She should never have been driving a car anyway. It's a wonder she didn't kill everyone on the road. She was crippled, after all, and crippled in the head to boot. The way she walked, that leg she dragged. And she also had a hand she couldn't control.

And she was a secret drunk. Sipped wine out of Pepsi bottles. In that last car wreck on Route One, the police didn't think anything of it at first while she was sitting there in the ditch, while her car burnt up, happily sipping out of a Pepsi bottle. They thought she was just high-steerical until they found out she was pie-eyed. They arrested her then for drunken driving and manslaughter.

She killed another man in one awful pile-up on the Taunton Bridge that laid her up in the hospital for months. Remember how Timmy was still a baby and he flew right out of Julie's arms off the bridge into the water? It was a miracle how that young policeman jumped in and saved him. Both of Julie's legs were broken, and in the hospital, they had her strapped up, hanging from the ceiling.

She was there in November when the Christmas wreath business had started and Garland tried to lug a bunch of tree branches into her hospital room so Julie could help him make some wreaths while she was laid up. They stopped him from doing that, though.

Garland worked harder than ever, after Julie got out of the hospital, to keep that little family of his together and going. He worked at the Taunton Tannery those years, before it shut down, as well as kept up with all of his little odd jobs all over town.

But Julie got crazier and crazier. The church tried to take her in for counseling two or three times, but that didn't work. She was too far gone by then and in and out of the Bangor Mental Hospital after that.

She wasn't stupid, though; but she was always much worse off than Garland.

Garland's not crazy, but she was.

He threatened to divorce her after he saw the size of her hospital bills; but she finally left him, which was really no big surprise. She got him to marry her, after all. The whole thing seemed to be her idea. Everyone expected her to go, probably even Garland. She went back to her folks over in Augusta some place. Took Timmy with her, which is sad, because Garland loved his little boy.

And he's normal and a real good kid, which proves that two wrongs can make a right.

Too bad he couldn't have stayed with his father and not his crazy mother.

Now Garland's more alone than ever.

He smells just like a fish factory. He must wear those rubber boots day and night.

The ballot clerks said that at last summer's special election Garland appeared with oilskins on all covered with mud. They couldn't get rid of him. He wanted to keep talking to them, so, finally, one of them told him that the clerks weren't supposed to talk to the voters. It was against the law during an election, so he trudged off.

Remember during the Sesquicentennial Church service, when the minister forgot to tell him that the service would start earlier at ten and not at the usual time of eleven? Garland was up on the altar vacuuming and not even noticing that the church was filling up with people.

And when he was told, remember how he looked around and about? Just like a queer bird, making strange jerky movements, as if to say, for God's sake, where am I? What are all these people doing here? It was so funny to see him crouched there on the altar. Finally, he clomped off the stage into the vestry, dragging the vacuum cleaner after him.

The saddest sight I ever saw was Garland at Dr. Bounty's funeral. Everyone went to that service because Dr. Bounty was so beloved around here. Garland was all dressed up in his good black suit sitting in a back pew, when at the end of the ceremonies when everyone was weeping and wailing, his former wife Julie and son Timmy, now grown up to be a good-looking boy, walked right by him. He turned towards them, grinning like a madman, with his hand stretched out to them; but they pretended not to notice him and walked right by, stuck up as can be. He stared and stared after them, not saying a word, his pleading grin slowly fading.

That was mean doing that to him.

Well, it just goes to show you what a thing she is to turn his son against him.

So many conversations in this town begin and end with Garland. He's almost like a flagpole or a thermometer, something that everyone can point to. Everybody's favorite fool, the butt of so many little jokes. All the Garland watchers get such a kick out of him, the funny way he stacks his wood for the winter, the way he keeps that old wreck of a Ford going, the way he changes the oil in his car by straddling it across the ditch in front of his house and then lying in the ditch under it, the way he paints his house in the dark, and the strange combinations of clothes he wears. His little comments are remembered and savored and repeated at parties. Whether he realizes it or not, Garland has often been the life of the party in this town.

Some say Garland Coffin is just like Jesus. He's so good to everybody. He works so hard at minimum wage and he gives of himself all the time. He never does anyone else any harm.

And yet someone's always crucifying him.

He's the town freak, and perhaps the only example of real purity we have around here.

I heard a story about him just the other day. That Page girl, whose father is the poundkeeper down at the lobster pound where Garland works now, said she came across Garland sweeping up the floor in the office and she told him what a good job he was doing.

"So glad you noticed," said Garland.

THE BOX SNIFFER

I HAD DRIVEN DOWN TO SPRUCE HARBOR to get some pickled wrinkles that Penny and Dean Carlisle had put up and saved for me. Penny's father is a fisherman and he always has plenty of wrinkles; and I love to eat them cold and pickled right out of the jar. It was a dismal, foggy Saturday in mid-March; and when I walked into their house, Penny had just gotten the two tow-headed kids off to bed for their afternoon nap. Husband and wife were sitting at the kitchen table.

In response to my opener of, "How are ya?" Penny said, "I've got cabin fever wicked bad."

"Doesn't your husband take ya out once in awhile?"

"Are you kidding? Except for the weekly jaunt into Ellsworth, we haven't been out for months. This is a hand-to-mouth existence, ya know."

Close on my heels was Benita Knowles, a neighbor friend of Penny's who used to work with her at the fish factory; and so it wasn't long before the four of us were seated around the kitchen table having coffee and Penny's homemade chocolate chip cookies and talking about life at the fish factory, where Benita still works, and where Dean and Penny first met.

"How did you meet *exactly*?" I asked.

"I was working on the cutters one day, and I threw a fish at him," Penny said.

"Pardon my ignorance, but what are the cutters?" I asked.

"You know those fish steaks you can buy in sardine cans?"

"Sure."

"Well, they run the big fish through the cutters, which are very sharp knives to make fish steaks. It's colder than hell in there. Dean was driving me crazy, and I just had to do something to get him to notice me."

"I noticed ya," said Dean.

"But ya didn't ask me out till I threw that fish at ya. I almost got fired because of Dean. I used to linger on my breaks and at lunch time so I could go see where he was and keep peeking at him."

"Did you have any competition from other women?"

"Not from the young ones as much as the old ones who protected him. He was living with Cassie, the floor lady, and she kept as close an eye on Dean as she did on us packers."

"Is that what you did — pack?"

"That was one of my jobs. I was on the packing line first; then later in casing up. I worked the cutters, too, and stenciled fiber."

"What's that?"

"Marking the boxes in the shipping room," said Dean. "Each batch of fish that comes in is given a number. When we're stenciling fiber, we mark down the lot number of the fish they're casing up."

"How did you get a job at the fish factory?" I asked Penny.

"My mother and aunt worked there, and so it was easy. Runs in the family — packing sardines. I always wanted to work more with the men, though, instead of with the women. They got to do other stuff and run around more while we females had to stay put, as usual, in one place. You know how that works — the men get the fun jobs."

"Yeah," said Dean interrupting, "I had such fun and sweet-smelling jobs as pollution control, working on the mustard sauce, and unloading the trucks and boats. In the tank room once, a rat even ran up my leg. That was one of the fun things that happened!"

Penny laughed. "Yes, those damn wharf rats!"

"How does the whole process work now?" I asked. "I only remember being in the old fish factory once when I was a kid."

"That the one that burned down?" asked Benita, who, for all the time she sat and talked with us, never removed her heavy winter coat.

"Yes, it was all wooden and dark in there; and smelled like you'd expect a fish factory to smell — to high heavens."

"Well, when they bring in a truck of fish today," said Dean, "they flush 'em out with a salt water hose right into the refrigerator tanks. There's an incline belt — the 'hurdy gurdy' they call it — that runs up to the overhead belt that goes over the top of the fish tanks. There's a man there who guards the gates; and when one tank is full, they open the gate to the next one. There are six tanks in all. Takes two men to unload and one to control the tanks. If the fish have to be held for some reason in the summer when it's hot, a brine solution is added to keep 'em."

"Does everyone get to do different jobs?"

"Sure, if you're there long enough, or young like we were just starting out. Some people stay on the same job forever, once they've found their niche, while others tend to switch around and get to know all aspects of the business."

"Yes, look at Della. She can do anything there, but because she's the Champion Sardine Packer of the State of Maine, that's all she does — pack. You ought to see her when tourist season starts. She goes into her 'famous rhythm,' rocking back and forth like crazy," said Penny.

"They all do," said Dean. "You have to develop a rhythm to be able to do the job. And sometimes if one woman's rhythm interferes with the woman's at the next table, they jab and cut each other with their scissors. You know, the scissors they use to cut the heads and tails off the sardines."

"My rhythm consisted of cutting my fingers every time Dean went by," said Penny.

"Don't they still tape their hands?" I asked.

"Yes, we still do," said Benita, who got a word in every now and then, "but those scissors are razor sharp. They can cut right through the tape. And most of the women work at a very fast clip."

"Good pun, Benita!" I said; and we all laughed.

"You have to get into your own little world if you're packing fish," said Penny. "They bitch all the time — and they love it. The goddamn fish is too big, too short, too soft. There's no such thing as a right-sized fish."

"That's true, all right," said Benita. "They like to fight and argue, too."

"Yes!" said Penny, who was really warming to her subject now. "If you want the front seat on the bus, shove it down the chum hole!"

"What do you mean?" I asked.

"When I was working on the line, some women, like Della the Champ, used to always try and outpack everyone else. Della would make herself sick if someone packed more than she did. She'd load up her table even when everyone else was ready to go home. She'd never take a full lunch break, because she'd have to hurry back and load up her table ahead of everyone else. Boy, would they bitch on the bus about that. They'd say, 'Christ, we're never gonna get out of here, because Della's loaded up her table again!' Most of us packed at about the same rate because we didn't want the slower gals to feel bad. Needless to say, I was never one to overload my table. As soon as it got close to quitting time, I'd shove everything down my chum hole, including whole fish."

"What's the chum hole?"

"That's the trough at the end of each table where the packers shove the cut-off heads and tails. The stuff goes out through the trough onto a conveyor belt into the chum truck."

"What do they do with it?"

"It's all trucked up to Rockland or Belfast some place where some Japanese factory makes it into fish meal," said Dean.

"You know what Della did once at the end of one packing season?" asked Benita. "She's such a sentimental old fool that she made everyone gather together on the last day in the packing room and sing 'May the Good Lord Bless and Keep You Till We Meet Again.' "

"Yes, I heard about that incident," said Penny. "God, how I hated working there, scooping up those awful fish off the belt onto the table hour after hour. The belts with the fish and the cans and chum all going in different ways so you get dizzy. I don't know how you can still keep it up, Benita."

"It beats being on the unemployment line," said Benita.

"Yes, I guess you're right," said Penny.

"What are the hours for a shift?" I asked Benita.

"Most everyone works from seven to three, or seven to four," she said, "which means that the women from way Downeast or up your way at Taunton have to get up about four a.m. to get the bus."

"And don't get home till it's six at night," said Penny. "I remember going to work in the dark and coming home in the dark."

"So how did the pollution control work, Dean?" I asked.

"It didn't," said Dean. "They succeeded in getting the solid waste out of the water with the screens, but the oil and the real pollutants they were supposed to get out, they didn't. We never could get the oil separator regulated correctly. The only thing that we did get right was the new fiberglass and plastic tanks. You can't use wooden tanks any more, because they're not clean. You can't keep 'em clean."

"The one thing they never clean out are the tubs the mustard sauce comes in," said Penny. "Dean was so cute when he was working the sauce. He got the stuff all over him."

"At least it wasn't as dangerous as your putting the peppers in the cans!"

"Peppers?"

"Yes," said Penny, "for the hot sardines that we sell down south and in Mexico. You never see 'em around here, unless you order 'em special. The peppers come in these gallon cans with pepper juice. The women who pack put the peppers in and you have to be sure and coat your hands with oil and wear gloves. And if you go to the bathroom, you have to remember to get the pepper juice off. Otherwise, you're going to have a terrible time! You can't even wash your hands in hot water because that makes it worse."

"One time, Loretta Rankin put some pepper juice all over one toilet seat in the women's bathroom," said Benita.

"God, is Loretta still there?" Penny asked.

"Sure. She'll never leave. That's her life. And I, for one, don't want her to leave as long as I'm there. She's a riot."

"That's one you should meet, An-day," said Penny.

"Why, because she's a riot?" I asked.

"I guess probably! She's the life of the party. She brings zest to a boring job. She's loud, crazy, singing all the time, playing jokes on everybody, especially the women. I'll never forget how she'd dance around and jazz the joint up. She'd poke people through the carriers and crawl under the coolers. She'd tickle anybody. One time she put dead rats in the coolers to get the women going."

"She caused a commotion last week when she pulled Dottie's pants down!" said Benita.

"How'd that happen?" said Penny.

"Dottie had these elastic-topped drawers on, and Loretta could hardly wait till Dottie was turned back to her. She snuck up on her and pulled 'em down. You should have heard Dottie scream. And what was funniest was that Dottie didn't have any underpants on! That was a riot."

"What is Loretta's job, beyond providing entertainment?"

"Oh, she's the head box sniffer!"

"What's that?"

"She sniffs the boxes that the cans are in to see if there are any bad ones. She's an expert sniffer."

"When does she get to do that?"

"Well, after all the sauces and peppers are put in the cans, they go onto the sealer," said Dean, "which is like a carousel. Then, they're cooked for the first time in steam boxes. The trays they're cooked on go on carts. They do two carts at a time; then the flake is removed from the tops of the carts, so they tip and the excess oil can be drained from the boxes. They're cooked for about fifteen or twenty minutes. The cans are then washed off on the way to the retorts, which are big pressure cookers, where they are cooked for a second time. After the retorts, they are cooled down. It takes two weeks for them to set. After two weeks, Loretta gets to sniff 'em. After they're sniffed, they carton 'em."

"You have to be careful of the 'puffs,' " Penny said. "Those are cans where the seal isn't proper. They swell up and they can blow up in your face. It's happened to Loretta. It's dangerous and poisonous. Some of the sniffers have got the stuff in their eyes after a puff has blown up."

"I used to work casing up," Penny continued, "which is a cleaner job with less women and less tension. There's a different atmosphere in there. The cans come on belts and drop into bins. We put 'em on a pallet which can hold twenty-four cases with fifty cans in a case. Of course, there are different sizes of cases, so it varies."

"Go back to the budding love affair. How did you pursue Dean, the handsome young stranger from away?"

"Oh, yes. In my pursuit of Dean, things did come to a head one day in the shipping room when we were all stenciling fiber. Dottie, the girl who just lost her drawers, and her sister Verna run that area. They're Della the Champ's daughters, so along with her, the three of them think they run the whole factory. Dottie was sort of the top girl in the shipping room and her and I got into it hot and heavy one afternoon. We were casing up by the big coolers where the boxes are kept before sniffing. Dottie and Verna were breaking in a new girl, when all of a sudden, Dottie just flew at me, hollaring, 'Now, look, ya little bitch; if you think you're going home before I do, you're wrong!' It was a bad day, one of those days when everything was rushed up and backed up. We were all hollaring for fiber. Just before she lit into me, Dottie run out of fiber, and A-Ball threw it at her and she called him a 'fucking son of a bitch.' "

"Who's A-Ball?"

"Oh, he's a nice quiet guy actually, who's like a gofer. They call him A-Ball, because he's supposed to only have one ball. Anyway, Dottie was fighting with me. All day she and Verna were at me, making their dirty little comments about my liking Dean, and how disappointed I was going to be when he ran off with someone else."

"So what happened?"

"Nothing ultimately. Verna did say to me, 'You think you're too good for the local guys around here. You gotta go for the guy from outa state.' She shut up when Loretta reminded her that she and Dottie had both married guys from the Navy base."

"Weren't people naturally intrigued by you, Dean, since you were a summer boy working here in the fish factory in the winter?"

"If they were," Dean said, "they didn't let on too much. They were mostly all pretty nice to me. I tried to do the jobs they gave me. I was there to learn and listen, after all."

"Yes, you were such a noble hero, de-ah," said Penny.

"Isn't there a lot of such gossip that goes on, just like in any place?" I asked.

"Of course!" said Benita. "That's what that place runs on — not fish oil — but gossip!"

"Hell, yes," said Penny. "The women gossip about the men, but I don't think the men do that quite so much; do they, de-ah?"

"Oh, on a break, and especially in the mornings, they would sit around on the tables telling fishing and clamming stories mostly. I never said much and neither did A-Ball, since he's a Witness."

"What's he a witness to?" I asked.

"Oh, he's a Jehovah's Witness. He did offer me some private advice, however, one day about Penny."

"What was that?"

"He told me I oughta take her out and screw her."

"Well, by God, A-Ball was right!" said Penny. "I'm glad that you finally got up enough courage to take his advice!"

A REAL ROUNDABOUT KIND OF GUY

I ONLY EVER KNEW Fredonna Wentworth from a distance. Coming and going from Ellsworth, I'd frequently see her, a ragged old bum dressed in mixed-match dresses and coats, picking up bottles beside the road. She'd be scavenging in the ditches along Route One, her face and head usually covered by a dirty scarf to protect, I presumed, her eyes and nose from the dust kicked up by the passing cars and trucks. In the winter time, or on rainy days, when one could catch a glimpse of her face, she looked gaunt and wrinkled and crazy. When she wasn't bent over combing the ditches, and just walking along toting her burlap sack full of her day's pickings, she'd stare right at the occupants of a car as if searching hard for a familiar face.

She'd be frequently joked about as I was growing up, but I never thought about her much, until one night recently when Aunt Bunny Crowley mentioned her and I asked her whatever became of Fredonna.

"The last time I remember seeing her around here," said Aunt Bunny, "was at a Maundy Thursday service one spring up at the Congregational Church. She came in and sat right behind us and cried all through the service. That's supposed to be a quiet service, ya know, so we were all disturbed. We even moved away from her finally. It was terrible. You could hear her sobbing all over the church. Mr. Higgins was the pastor at that time and he did what he could for her, but she was pretty far gone at that point."

"I remember seeing her alongside the road, picking up bottles. She looked like the town bum," I said.

"Well, she was, but not early on."

"She used to sort of stumble along Route One, and you couldn't help but notice her because she was so strange acting."

"Well, she walked backwards. Don't you remember?"

"Yes, I guess she did."

"She was also crazy as a loon. She was in and out of mental hospitals after her mother died and her husband ran off."

"I never knew she was married."

"Oh, yes."

"Was she born here?"

"Born and brought up. Over on the West Side in the old Merrill place. Her father was Clyde Wentworth. He worked down to The Point, like everyone else. He did odd jobs for the summer people and always wore the same sport coat year-round. Even though the summer people gave him all kinds of clothes, he still wore the same coat."

"Don't you remember her mother, old Mrs. Wentworth?" asked Aunt Bunny.

"Was she the little old hunched-over woman who wore long black dresses and a black hairnet down over her forehead, and walked with a cane?"

"Yes. She was like a little old witch. They say she kept her knitting in the refrigerator."

"What became of Clyde?"

"Everyone was shocked when Clyde Wentworth shot himself to death with a deer rifle out in his woodshed."

"Why?"

"Nobody knows. He just did one night. We all went over to examine the bullet hole that went right through his head and through the back shed door. It's probably still there."

"Well, I don't think I'll bother to run right over and check."

"Right after Clyde did himself in, Fredonna and her mother really blossomed out. They got themselves a brand new car and spruced up their old house."

"How come? Did Clyde leave some money?"

"I should say so! Over $50,000, I heard. And no one could figure out how he had accumulated so much because all he ever did was work down on The Point mowing lawns, painting, and being a caretaker; and you know as well as I do you don't get rich working for these summer people we've got around here."

"Maybe he was into rum-running?"

"He only had a rowboat; and he didn't have a truck. You had to have a good boat or truck for that trade."

"Tell more. I want to hear the whole story."

"Well, I don't know the whole story, but I remember that it was soon after Fredonna had come into her inheritance and was living it up with her old mother, when Hank Tattersall came to town to work down on Dana Stevens' farm with the cows. Pretty soon, we'd see Fredonna and Hank driving all over town in Fredonna's new car. She had a big one, too; I think it was a Buick or a Chrysler. Real fancy; and they went everywhere. Finally, they got married."

"What was Hank like?"

"Oh, he was a real roundabout kind of guy. Everyone liked him. He was good looking and awfully nice spoken. Worked hard on the farm. Had a good sense of humor. Dana always spoke well of him. Everyone was pleased for Fredonna at that point. They lived together for almost a year, when Hank took off with all her money."

"They never caught him? Fredonna didn't go after him?"

"They couldn't trace him. Everyone was astounded that such a nice feller as Hank would up and do such a thing. I don't know where he was from originally. Massachusetts, I think. Hank was very nice to Fredonna's mother."

"So what happened to Fredonna after that?"

"Well, she was back where she started from, only worse. I don't know whether she cracked up then or not, because your Uncle Gene and I were away all those years working as a maid and butler team down on the Island and then in Boston. I was only home once in a while, so I lost track of Fredonna. You'd have to ask someone else who was here all the time to fill ya in on those years."

"Well, what happened to her mother?"

"She died; and I think it was probably right after that that Fredonna had her first big breakdown. She was never too strong physically or mentally, but she did put up a nice stone for her mother in the graveyard."

"But wasn't she related to the Wentworths, the first family of Taunton? Didn't they help her out? They certainly had plenty of money."

"Fredonna was adopted. And her father was kind of the black sheep of the Wentworth family. I'm not sure why, except that he was a loner and kind of a bum himself, always wearing that same old sport coat. He never had much to do with his relatives, as far as I know."

"So Fredonna was alone and penniless."

"Well, I suppose she sold her parents' place, or lost it, I don't know."

"Did she build that shack she lived in at the crossroads between old Route One and new Route One?"

"Well, she sure didn't hire any Bangor architect! It was erected out of odds and ends, mostly odds, I'd say. No one ever knew how she kept warm in that joint."

"What I thought was clever was the way she got that old Sunoco sign because of its angular shape to fit next to the roof."

"Yes, remember how your Uncle Gene used to tell summer tourists to be sure and stop at the new Sunoco station at the crossroads!"

"Yes! I hope some of them did."

"Oh, there is something else about Fredonna that I remember," said Aunt Bunny.

"What?"

"The way she loved going to funerals. She always dressed up then and always brought a single flower with her, which she'd usually hand to someone after the services. I remember seeing her standing at your Uncle Gene's funeral with a single glad in her hand. Without saying anything, she came over to me and gave me the glad! She'd go to all the funerals, whether she was invited or not and whether she knew the people or not."

"Her shack burnt down, didn't it?"

"Yes, and then she moved to Ellsworth, where she could really entertain herself with two funeral homes and a dozen churches. She used to make people mad, because when they'd pull up for a service, there would be crazy Fredonna peeking in the car windows at the bereaved. She wanted to share their grief, I guess. Don't you remember when she appeared at your father's funeral?"

"Yes, I do. I wasn't sure who she was at first, because she was all dressed up. She walked around and stared at all of us. My mother told her to go away."

"Did you know that Fredonna finally moved right into one of the funeral homes?"

"No, how so?"

"They had an apartment upstairs they used to rent out, and that's really the last I ever heard about her. She moved into the funeral home and was never seen again. Maybe they buried her by accident! She was so weird, so in love with death, that I bet she went downstairs at night and examined the dead bodies."

"Aunt Bunny, that's gory."

"Yes, of course it is; but that's the way Fredonna was. She was one of the living dead."

MISS GLOVER VISITS CLASS

THE PLAIN BLACK CHEVY two-door sedan would pull up right in front of the Taunton Ferry two-room schoolhouse where I attended kindergarten and the first four grades, and all of us kids knew what that meant: another regular visit by Nurse Kyle Glover, the school union's guardian of our health. Since there were six other grammar schools in our union, she only dropped by our educational institution of lower learning every two weeks or so and we never knew whether it was to be a five-minute lecture on dental care or an all-day affair called "Health Day." The teachers often didn't know either. Sometimes she weighed us, checked our vaccinations and temperatures, gave us some information to take home to our parents, or depressed our tongues and made us say, "Ah." Sometimes she lectured us on what we should eat for breakfast (I remember her particularly recommending Wheatena and Ralston); and once a year she gave us a hearing test by standing in the back of the room and whispering. If we could hear her, we weren't deaf. Infrequently she showed us a movie. One I vividly recall, perhaps it was the first film I ever saw in school, was a technicolor film which showed people eating delicious desserts and then there was a microscopic close-up, done in cartoon style, of the food going into the people's mouths and down into their bodies, showing how the bodies' chemicals and digestive system processed all of the different foods.

Miss Glover had curly gray hair cut close to her head and wore rimless glasses. She always wore her navy blue rayon outfit with matching navy blue beanie with her nurse's pin attached to it. When she walked up and down the aisles we could hear her "whispering nylons" as well as the swish of her rayon uniform. She seemed to be always smiling and she was "officially kind" to all of us children; and very efficient and business-like in her manner. She tolerated no nonsense; that we understood from the first. No one gave her any trouble. When she entered the classroom, the teacher was relegated to being her assistant. She was convinced that her mission was supreme; and that our very lives depended upon our paying complete attention to her every word. We could never imagine Miss Glover relaxing at home or having any fun. If she had been a Catholic, she would probably have been a nun, for she did seem like one in her devotion to duty. Her life was, in fact, her nursing.

Being a relatively poor, rural Maine town, we had our share of bad health problems; and at the time, post World War II of the late 1940's, everyone was especially concerned about polio. The most popular radio announcer in Bangor at the time — Johnny MacCrae on WABI — took as his personal cause the sad case of polio victim Ebbie Brooks, a Maine teenager confined to an iron lung. There were practically daily messages to and from Ebbie at the Eastern Maine General Hospital; and special request songs were played over the radio, especially during the March of Dimes campaigns. Because of Mr. MacCrae's efforts, Ebbie became famous in Eastern Maine and a symbol of polio's dread crippling effects. Miss Glover even mentioned Ebbie Brooks in her little lectures to us on the summer dangers of swimming in stagnant frog ponds or quarries. The day Ebbie died, Nurse Glover was in our school and had us say a prayer for him.

There were two epileptics at the Taunton Ferry School when I was there. One was a girl, Glenda, and one was a boy, Peter. Both were nice kids and Glenda was one of the smartest students in the school; but there wasn't the medication there is today to help control their seizures, so both of them often had fits in front of all of us in the classroom, out on the playground, or on the schoolbus. I remember one time we were on the bus going on a field trip, and one of the kids sitting up back yelled at Gus Francis, the bus driver, "Gus! Glenda's having a fit!" We all turned around and there was Glenda down on her hands and knees in the aisle, looking wild-eyed, sick, and drooling. Gus pulled the bus to the side of the road, came back to where Glenda was, helped her outside of the bus, where he tried to pull her tongue out so she wouldn't swallow it. Naturally, we kids, a few of us laughing, all tried to peek out the windows to watch, but we couldn't see much. To his credit, Gus never allowed us to get off the bus at such times to stand around and gawk. At school, Nurse Glover always had private little talks with Glenda and Peter, showing special concern for them.

One time she told us about a little girl in Maine who got an awful huge splinter in her leg from sliding on a teeter totter at school, but who would never tell her teacher or anyone, not even her parents at home. This imbedded splinter later infected her leg so that it had to be amputated. The moral was, I guess, that we should always immediately tell someone of our accidents and get help.

"Don't be scared, boys and girls," she always said, "of nurses and doctors. We're only here to help you."

Since we had no running water nor any indoor bathroom at school, just an outdoor privy out back of the school building, Nurse Glover was forever telling us about the importance of good, clean toilet hygiene.

There was this very overweight girl in my class, Myrna Bridges, who was a diabetic and always giving herself injections of insulin right at her desk in school. She'd do this even when the teacher was teaching; and needless to say, all eyes were on Myrna, who took a great deal of time preparing herself and us for her ritual. It was really her claim to fame. At the height of the drama, she'd finally shove the needle in her arm, and we'd all gasp. "I've got to do this every day, or I'll die!" she told us. Covered with freckles, Myrna also had a special picture taken of herself with all of her freckles removed, which we all passed around the room and marveled at. When Nurse Glover was weighing us, one at a time, up in front of the classroom, we'd always take bets on how much Myrna weighed this time. "Myrna, you've just got to start cutting down," Miss Glover would say. Myrna was not a very good student and she was completely un-coordinated in games and sports. One winter we had this old, round Coca Cola sign we used to slide on down a hill near the school; and one time Myrna was right in the way and we flattened her. It took the rest of recess to dig her out of the snow.

Even worse off than Myrna was Eugene, a boy in my class, who had a huge head shaped like a watermelon standing on end. His hair was always matted and never washed. He was probably severely retarded, but we didn't know about special education in those days. He went to school right along with the rest of us. He'd sleep through most classes and always be wetting his pants so there'd be a puddle around his seat at the end of the day. Once in a while, a teacher would take a chance and call on Eugene; and he'd rise up, look about him as if dazed, not knowing exactly where he was. "Go back to sleep,

Eugene," one of our teachers was always saying. When we were in the eighth grade, Eugene was home one night cleaning a shotgun or playing with it and accidentally blew his head off.

One of the most pathetic cases of child neglect and abuse in my class that I recall was that of Mattie Carrington, a tiny, big-eyed, stringy-haired little girl who looked like one of the victims of Hitler's concentration camps. She was a bag of bones in a dirty, ragged dress. She was always twitching and scratching in her seat, looking as if she had some awful disease. One day when Nurse Glover was visiting our class, she said, "Boys and girls, Mattie has no lunch. I think it would be nice if you all shared some of your lunches with her." Since most of us never liked all the stuff our mothers packed in our lunches anyway, and because of the power of Miss Glover's appeal, we piled up our sandwiches and cookies on Mattie's desk, so much so that they were falling on the floor. I'll never forget the sight of seeing her greedily stuffing all the food in a paper bag, like some wild starving animal. It wasn't long after that incident that we read in the newspaper how Mattie's mother, who had several other children and lived in North Taunton in an abandoned tourist cabin, was arrested for feeding her kids out of garbage pails.

Several more such families in Taunton were dirt poor, and I suppose some might say degenerate, too. In any case, the children of one very destitute family, the Greels, never had a chance. They were blamed for all the crime and anything that ever went wrong with the town almost before they were grown up. Gus, the bus driver, would stop in the mornings by their tar-paper shack, sometimes toot the horn, and wait for a few minutes; and then, if there were no sign of a stirring within, drive on. When they'd all come to school, there was a Greel in every grade. When they'd get on the bus, some of the kids would hold their noses and yell, "Pee You! Greels! Greels! Back of the bus! Back of the bus!" But on their way back, the Greel boys would strike out at all of us with their dinner pails, rulers, whatever they had. And I never blamed them. Even when I got hit, I remember feeling that we deserved it. The whole scene always made me cringe and feel awful. It wasn't fair towards them and I always felt sorry for those kids. But I never said anything, and I never became friends with any of them.

In school, Nurse Glover singled out the Greels for public humiliation. She was forever telling them about personal hygiene and how they didn't have any, how bad they always smelled. One time she brought in a fine-toothed steel comb with which to comb hair for lice. Since the Greels were half-breeds, and all had thick long hair, Miss Glover announced to the class that she was checking for lice, and she actually started combing one of the Greel girl's hair in my class; but she stopped when the girl shoved her away, screaming, "Leave me alone, you old bitch! Don't you touch my hair with that damn comb!"

Nurse Glover, and most of us kids, was shocked by anyone, especially a student, daring to challenge her authority in such a crude manner with such filthy language. "Now, listen here, my girl, we can't have you spreading your lice around here!"

"I ain't your girl, you old bitch! And I ain't spreading no bugs around this goddamn school! You leave me alone!"

Surprisingly, she did; and our teacher, who was a much more compassionate and humane woman, came over to comfort the girl, who was shaking and sobbing, and helped her from the classroom.

Nurse Glover did manage to compose herself once again and say a few more words about the danger of lice in our hair; but she didn't do any more combing that day, and never again in the classroom, as I recall. She left; and I think we were all relieved. As for the Greel girl, she didn't come back to school for over two weeks; but I certainly wasn't very surprised.

QUEERS IN THE WOODS

IT WAS LATE JUNE. I was over to Britt's Department Store in the Ellsworth Shopping Center trying to purchase a black-and-white Instamatic film for my camera, because I wanted to get some pictures of the guy I was going to interview that afternoon for the local newspaper I then worked for. The only film they had, however, was colored, so I had to buy that, knowing it wouldn't reproduce as well in the newspaper. My sixteen-year-old nephew Randy, sort of named for me, was with me. He had been living with my mother and me all spring, having been sent up to Maine from Florida where my brother worked at Cape Kennedy and where Randy had gotten into drugs and trouble. He had just completed his sophomore year, more or less, in high school. We were supposed to be keeping an eye on him and life in Maine was supposed to be helping to reform him and to be exposing him to those good old Yankee values that come from a life full of struggle, hard work, individualism and honesty. The type of values my older brother thought he had from having grown up here. While I was at the camera display and film counter area, Randy had wandered off to the record and stereo section. He rejoined me at carside, and we took off. I hadn't driven for more than a mile down the road when Randy said, "Hey, Uncle Andy. These stores here in Maine are sure easy to rip off."

"Why do you say that?" I asked, remembering Randy's Florida troubles and my mother's accusing him of stealing her Sunday paper money from the jar on the kitchen sideboard.

"Look." I looked over at him in the other bucket seat and he was hauling cassette tapes out of the front of his jeans. "I got four new ones," he said.

"Randy! Why did you steal them?"

"I wanted to."

"If you wanted them so bad, why didn't you ask me for the money?"

"Would you have given it to me?"

"Probably not, but maybe for one of them. You know, your grandmother and I live here. We know everyone and everyone knows us. You just can't go into places like that and rip them off."

I should have swung the car around right then and driven back to Britt's and made him go with me back into the store and return the tapes; but I didn't want to make a federal case out of it. I was trying to reach him, after all, by befriending him. I wanted him to trust me, so I could perhaps reform him that way. But in the back of my mind I knew I shouldn't let such an incident go by and just let him off with my little ineffectual lecture.

"I should turn this car around, go back, and turn you in."

"So why don't you?"

"I'm ashamed and embarrassed."

"You're also in a big hurry to go interview this guy."

"That's right; and that's why I won't turn back this time, but I would like your promise to me that you'll never do this again while you are here. Are your habits so ingrained that you can't change?"

"What does 'ingrained' mean?"

"So strong that you can't change?"

"No. I know it's wrong."

"Then, why do you do it?"

"All the kids do it."

"That's no reason."

Randy was a very handsome boy, just like my brother had been. He was tall with an athletic build. He had no acne and his skin always seemed tan. He had long brown hair with big brown eyes. When he smiled his face lit up. He was a pretty boy, in the All-American Hollywood sense. He had so many girlfriends, even after having only been in Maine for a few months, that the phone never stopped ringing. Older women, too, were always praising his looks and calling him a "real cutie." Because of all this attention, even at sixteen, he already thought of himself as a superstud. He reminded me of a line from Tennessee Williams about how a boy like that need never go hungry. All he had to do was wear tight pants on the street. And that's how Randy always dressed: tight jeans, his tapered shirt open halfway to his waist, a gold chain around his neck.

We talked of sex.

"I'm not a virgin, ya know, Uncle Andy."

"Now, when, Randy, did you lose your virginity?"

"Thirteen. You remember that lady who lived next door to my father's house in Florida — Mrs. Benign?"

"Not really. I was never there long enough in all my visits to get to know the neighbors."

"Well, she sure was something. She was married, but once, when her husband was gone, she invited me over to her house."

"And so she seduced you?"

"What?"

"Seduced means she invited you to have sex with her?"

"Yes."

"How old was this madam?"

"Oh, twenty-eight or thirty or so. She had kids."

"Well, I don't now whether that was a good idea, or whether she should have been arrested for contributing to the delinquency of a minor."

"It wasn't delinquent. It was great! We did it all the time after that. She said I was handsome and she loved my looks. She also said I was a terrific lover."

"Did your parents know about this?"

"No, and please don't tell them."

"Did you smoke pot with her, too?"

"Sure. She was a very cool, very together lady. I'd like to meet someone like her again. I'd just move right into her bedroom and never move out."

"That would sure beat working for a living, wouldn't it? You know, Randy, looks like yours are important, but they are not everything."

"They sure help ya get some nice chicks."

"Yes, I suppose they do; there's no question that good looks are an initial asset in matters of sex; but as your schoolteaching uncle who sent you books for every birthday and Christmas, I want you to be good at more than just intercourse."

"I don't see what's better than intercourse!"

"You could be living a richer, fuller life."

"By reading books? Like you? Listen, Uncle Andy, I don't mean to insult you, but your life looks boring to me. I think sex and money and having fun is what life's all about."

We talked of sports. "Why did you quit the baseball team this spring?"

"The stupid coach wanted me to cut my hair! And I told him, no way, Jose!"

"But you're a good player, Randy, a natural athlete like your father. You quit football down in Florida, too, didn't you?"

"Yes, but that was the niggers! The coach was black and he always favored the black guys. I was always getting knocked around by those niggers!"

"Did you ever think that it might have been your attitude? You do swagger around, you know, like you're a big macho stud, daring people to take you on."

"I beat this one nigger up so bad that I got a reputation just before I left Florida that no one was to mess with me."

"And now, you're getting a reputation around here in Maine."

"How so?"

"That incident in the high school when you were caught with a girl on the floor of the boys' bathroom."

He laughed. "I just couldn't help it, Uncle Andy! That girl was something else! Best piece I've had up here in Maine. You should meet her; she's great."

"Yes, I imagine, any girl who would screw boys on the floor of a toilet is a very winsome lass."

"What's a 'winsome lass?' "

"A charming young lady."

"Well, she is."

"Randy, I'm just glad that Ben Harlow, your English teacher and my friend, caught you that time. It could have been a much worse situation if it had been, say, the principal."

"I still got suspended."

"And rightly so. Don't you remember that talk with me and the guidance counsellor about taking some responsibility for your sex life?"

"Sure."

"Did what we said to you sink in at all?"

"I think it was all blown out of proportion, a big deal out of nothing."

"No, then I guess it didn't sink in. You know you hurt your grandmother very much over that little scene. She's very proud and has lived all of her life around here. She was disgusted that one of her grandsons would do such a thing."

"How did she find out?"

"People do. That's what I'm trying to tell you. You can't keep something like that secret in a small town area. Someone will talk, and they tell someone else. It's too juicy a story to keep quiet about. Your grandmother was ready at that point to ship you back to Florida."

"Well, I wish she had. Florida's much better than Maine."

"In what way?"

"In all ways. It's so boring around here. You have to hitchhike ten miles to go shopping. All Maine people do is work, go to bed early, talk funny, and watch 'Stacy's Country Jamboree'! They don't know how to party. They're uncool. There's much more going on down in Florida. And it's too damn cold around here!"

By this time, I had driven from Ellsworth to West Hamlin, off Route One, to the Turnip Hill Road, on which I used to run cross country when I was Randy's age at nearby Mollusk Memorial High. When we came to the end of the dirt road, I parked the car and we continued on foot along an old woods trail through the thick underbrush, so alive and green, especially alive with black flies.

"Jesus, Uncle Andy! We should have covered ourselves with some bug stuff!"

"I doubt it would have done much good. We'll just have to walk fast and keep slapping them away as best we can."

And so we did. Running and hollaring through the woods, slapping our faces, and waving the air with our hands and arms. I was carrying my notebook and a bottle of sauterne to help oil the interview. Randy carried the camera.

"Who is this guy anyway?" Randy asked.

"He's a Maine author who has written a couple of fine books which I reviewed. I heard he was living in this old camp up here for the summer, and I thought he might make a good interview subject."

"Well, I hope it's worth being bitten to death by these damn flies."

The trail seemed to peter out after about a mile into the woods, and barely discernible down near a small brook was this dilapidated old hunting camp.

"I think this is the place," I said.

"God, I hope so," said Randy. "I hope he's got some screens on the windows and all the holes in this joint plugged up."

I knocked on the door, and, to my surprise, and probably even more to Randy's, a thin-faced, skinny, sensitive-looking young black man, attired in cut-off jeans and sandals, opened the door.

"Yes?" he asked.

"I'm sorry to disturb you, but I was told Mr. Philip Hammond, the author, was living here for the summer."

He smiled. "Yes, you're right he is, but I'm afraid he's not here right now. He went down to the village for some groceries. Since we don't have a refrigerator, we have to go every day. But he should be back soon. You're welcome to come in and wait for him."

"All right, we will. It will be good to get away from these black flies," I said, realizing suddenly that I had said the word "black" and hoped that that is what he also called the miserable pests.

"Yes, they are the worst thing about this camp."

"I'm Andy Griffin, incidentally, and I write for an Ellsworth newspaper. I want to interview Mr. Hammond about his writing."

"It's nice to meet you; I'm Rudolph Patterson, a good friend of Mr. Hammond's."

Up to this point, I hadn't dared look at Randy.

"This is Randy, my nephew."

They shook hands and Randy smiled timidly.

"Hi," he said.

"Now," said Mr. Patterson, chuckling, "we don't entertain much. As you can see, there is only one chair, which is in rather deplorable condition. We don't have many of the comforts of home. We are roughing it for the summer."

There was only one room in the camp. Besides the chair, there was a mattress upon which both occupants evidently slept with pillows and a tangle of blankets and sheets. There was a typewriter and a transistor radio-recorder with some tapes. Books, magazines, dishes, and old clothes were scattered and piled everywhere. There was a rusty old sink in one corner next to an equally rusty wood stove; but there didn't seem to be any running water and no electricity. Three little gray kittens were playing in another corner. I sat in the deplorable chair, Randy squatted on the floor, and our kindly host, a golden earring dangling from his left ear, crouched on the mattress. Randy picked up one of the kittens to play with while Rudolph and I proceeded to discuss the works of Mr. Hammond, the wonders of the Maine Coast, and ultimately race relations. I told him about some of my experiences as a teacher in a racially-troubled Syracuse high school in the late 1960's and early 1970's; and he told me about the problems of growing up black in South Boston.

After over a half-hour or so had elapsed, and still no Mr. Hammond, I suggested we drink some of the wine. Both Rudolph and Randy readily agreed. Rudolph provided clean paper cups and I poured. The wine helped, and after awhile, even Randy became more his animated self, talking about his Florida and Maine high school experiences. I was proud of him that he was so polite and carried on a decent conversation entirely devoid of bigotry or racial slurs.

However, it became apparent, after an hour more, and with the wine gone, that Mr. Hammond had probably gone shopping further than West Hamlin village, perhaps as far as Ellsworth, as his friend suspected; and so we took our leave.

"It was great meeting you," I said to Rudolph.

"I'm sorry, though, that you went to all this trouble for no interview," Rudolph said.

"I should have interviewed you," I said. "You're a very interesting man."

"Thank you," he said, and to Randy, "Well, good-bye, Randy. Good luck to you."

"Thanks. Goodbye," said Randy.

"Look, I'll tell Phil," said Rudolph, "when he gets back about your visit and have him call you to see about arranging a meeting; but be forewarned that he may not consent."

"I understand," I said. "Thank you again, and I would appreciate it if you could arrange something."

"I'll try."

He waved to us as we went down the path and through the trees, back to slapping black flies again.

"Honest to God, Uncle Andy," said Randy. "Was that nigger queer or what?"

"I don't know, Randy; but I was proud of the way you conducted yourself back there, and now, here you are using insulting words like 'nigger' and 'queer' again! Calling people names!"

"Well, he has to be a queer to live with another guy like that, sleeping together, wearing an earring, talking fancy like he did, and staring all the time at my crotch!"

"At least you could say 'homosexual,' and not 'queer.' How would you like to be called names?"

"I am! 'Stupid!' 'Jerk-Off!' 'Pretty Boy!' 'Flunk Out!' Those are the names I'm called."

"Along with 'racist,' 'bigot,' and 'thief'!"

"Well, at least I ain't no goddamn queer!"

"At least. Oh, God, look! One of the little kitties has followed us."

Randy bent down to pick up the little, purring gray fellow. "This is the one I was playing with. He's a male. A tom cat! See his balls! He didn't want to stay anymore with those queers in the woods, so he followed us!"

"Yes, especially since he caught a whiff of your irresistible crotch!"

"Let's take him. We can't go back there now with him, Uncle Andy, so let's take him with us. I'll raise him to be a mean, fighting tom. Besides, they've got two left."

"Why not! Take him with your hot cassettes, and we'll stop by the West Hamlin Grocery and you can run in and rip off some cat food. You can tuck it in your jeans; and then we can go find your dope pusher in Ellsworth and get higher than we already are, with Kitty, laid back like down to Florida listening to all your cool tunes!"

"Now you're talking, Uncle Andy!"

MRS. LAWSON ARRIVES FOR THE SUMMER

MOST GUESTS DIDN'T ARRIVE at Frenchman's Bay Manor like Julie Lawson by trying to drive their car through a cedar hedge. Most also didn't park their cars in the servants' back parking lot and fraternize so much with the help. Julie did, though, and I was glad because she made me laugh and I liked her.

It was early afternoon when she arrived in July in her 1956 two-tone blue Ford Fairlane, but her conservative choice in cars was misleading, to say the least.

I was just finishing up the luncheon pots and pans when Julie flounced, because she never just walked, into the kitchen.

"Hi!" she breathlessly exclaimed, bouncing up and down on her toes; but because she came in the back way, I wasn't sure if she were to be accorded guest status or what.

She was so girlish-acting, even though one could see from her graying brown curly hair that she was not really young. She was dressed in blue flared trousers with white blouse and sneakers. Her hair was pulled back by her ears. She was tanned and pretty, and looked like she had just been sailing. She radiated energy and seemed never still, always moving about. She jounced across the kitchen on her toes to greet Miss Meyer, the owner of the Manor and my boss.

"Jean! . . . so good!" she said, taking Miss Meyer's hands in hers and holding them for what seemed an inordinate amount of time, all the while looking into Miss Meyer's face, giggling through a smile which lit up her face, but saying nothing more, as if she were too overcome for words.

"Errr," said Miss Meyer, who always cleared her throat before speaking, "it's good to have you back, Julie." My boss then pulled her hands away, but all the same trying to be naturally friendly, which was hard for her. Perhaps she had been an old maid secretary in New York for too many years. She always was awkward and mannered, particularly when greeting someone as effervescent as Julie Lawson.

But Julie didn't seem to mind or notice any such awkwardness. "So good," she repeated in her whispery voice; and then she tip-toed across the kitchen to me. "Hi!" she exclaimed again, extending her hand. My hands had been in the dishpan, and she didn't give me time to wipe them, but she didn't seem to mind the suds. She seized upon my right hand and squeezed it, looking like a little girl discovering something brand new and exciting. "You're the new boy!" she said.

"Yes," I said.

"Errr . . . his name is Andy," said Miss Meyer.

"Andy," Julie repeated with what I determined had to be a southern accent. "Will you help me . . . when you can?" she asked in a pleading tone.

"What?" I asked in return, not understanding exactly what she meant. I found out soon enough that Mrs. Lawson hardly ever completed her sentences when she talked. And her fragmented speech was often vague and inexplicit. She evidently expected people to garner the gist of her communication through osmosis.

"Errr . . . he's about done and will be right out to help you, Julie," Miss Meyer said, clearing the whole matter up.

"Good!" Julie exclaimed, for she was full of exclamations. "I'll go, and Andy will come . . ." She started to tip-toe away, only to run into Hattie, the head waitress, emerging from the dining area.

"Hattie!" she whooped, bouncing over to her, giggling and taking her by the hand, saying, "I'm back! You're here!"

Hattie laughed and said, "Yes, I guess we both are. Ready to go another round, Julie. It's good to see ya."

"I need your help, Hattie," said Julie.

"I know it, Julie, you always have."

"Will you sew?" Julie asked.

"When I get time. What do you need sewed?"

"Things. Many little things. Everything's falling apart."

"Don't I know it!" Hattie exclaimed.

"Good, you'll sew then?" Julie turned to leave, "You'll come, Andy? I'll be by the trunk."

"Yes, right away," I said, assuming that she referred to her car's trunk, not that of an elephant, tree, or steamer, but not altogether sure. She did seem magical, after all.

"Is there juice, Jean?" Julie asked Miss Meyer from the doorway.

"Errr . . . there's some orange. Could I get you a glass?"

"Please! I need it. The trip was hot . . . I could drink a jug!"

She had two tall glasses of orange juice which she seemed to relish as her life's blood, giggling at all three of us, and looking wild-eyed about the kitchen, while she sipped from her glass. Then, all of a sudden, finished, she plunked down the empty glass, jumped up, and danced out of the room.

"Well, An-day, was that your first real-life glimpse of a tip-toeing southern belle?" Hattie asked.

"I guess so. You both had mentioned her, but I didn't really expect anyone so . . ."

"Nuts?" Hattie asked. "Listen, if she didn't have the millions she's supposed to, they'd lock her up in a padded cell. You ain't seen nothing yet, honey chile!"

"Why does she walk on her toes?"

"She's floating on air — the air between her ears, that is! But don't worry; she tips, when you remind her what planet she's on."

"Errr . . . you'd better go help her now," Miss Meyer suggested, evidently wishing to discourage any more of Hattie's comments concerning the Manor's longest-paying, full-season guest.

"Yais, and go easy with the hoop skirts, high protein cereals, and magnolia blossoms, An-day, hon-ay," mocked Hattie, executing a tip-toeing imitation of Mrs. Lawson back to the dining room.

Peering into the trunk of Mrs. Lawson's Ford, I was curious to see how she packed, or didn't pack, as the case seemed to be. There was only one old battered suitcase; everything else, including underwear and melted chocolates, was wrapped in plastic or paper bags or in newspaper or just lying free on top of everything else. The rear seat had been removed and therein lay more of the same: another battered suitcase, a half-dozen floppy wide-rimmed picture hats, one with little red balls decorating its rim, half-eaten boxes of "health" candy, petticoats, bundles of dead, dry foliage, magazines, books, swim suits, bottles of lotion, and a partial set of weights.

"Trunk first," Mrs. Lawson said, beginning to remove things from the rear of the car and placing them in little piles on top of and beside the Ford. As I began to help her, I noticed what looked to be an expensive cocktail dress stuffed about the spare tire as if it were used to wipe some grease monkey's hands.

"Oh, it's bad," she said, "do you know someone who cleans?"

"My mother. She takes in washings."

"Good. Could you take it to her?" She held the greasy gown out to me. "And does she sew? Mrs. Pinkham's always so busy . . ." Mrs. Pinkham was Hattie.

"So is my mother," I said to myself. "Yes, she does, and very well."

"Then, I have a few things," she said.

She held up a piece of white canvas which turned out to be a cloth helmet cut to fit her head when swimming. "I can't have the sun strike my face when I'm in the pool," she explained. "But I need wider nose holes and mouth opening. I nearly choked and drowned last week."

It looked to me like the Phantom's head covering; I was thinking to myself what my mother would say when she saw this. She was always joking over what "little jobs" the summer people had her do, like the time Ambassador Sedgwick's wife brought her Burmese draperies to my mother to be made into a gown. It was amusing to me, imagining Mrs. Lawson with her canvas helmet on at the Taunton Point Pool down the street, midst all the royal blood.

She also handed me a ripped pea green bathing suit for my mother to sew; and then we began the unpacking of the car in earnest. She busily tried to arrange and organize her stuff into little piles about the car and parking lot while I began transporting things upstairs to her room where I was instructed to make other little piles. At one point, I was carrying a bag of Florida oranges, a make-up kit, a bottle of Poland Spring Water, and a plastic bag of bathing suits.

All during this process, which took over an hour, and which more or less continued throughout the rest of the summer, she would pause and ask me questions about my health and hobbies.

"Let me see your teeth," she said.

I did as I was commanded, and she put her hand into my mouth and examined my teeth, finally declaring, "They seem strong. Are they?"

"I think so. I've only had about two cavities ever."

"Do you chew?"

"Things that need chewing."

"Chewing is good. Chew always."

"Do you break bones?" she asked.

"No, not if I can help it."

"Don't drink Coke," she said, and returned to her unpacking.

After the car, she told me to go up into the attic and fetch a steamer trunk she kept there filled with her summer frocks.

"I purchased these dresses in New York in 1948 for my first season here . . . it's been twelve seasons, but they'll still do fine. Isn't this one lovely?" She held up this light green, full-skirted, padded-shouldered monstrosity for my praise.

"Yes," I said, convinced of her insanity, and waiting, now that the errands had been done, to see if there would be any tip.

"Ohhh!" she finally exclaimed, rushing to her pocketbook on her dresser, fumbling through it, scattering credit cards, twenty and fifty dollar bills, finally handing me a five, the biggest tip I had ever received from a summer guest up till then.

"Here!" she said, crumpling the bill into my hand. "From a very grateful Mrs. Lawson."

"Thank you," I said. "See you later."

"Ummmm," she hummed, smiling her funny little quivering smile, closing the door behind me.

I returned to the kitchen and there sat Hattie and Miss Meyer having a cigarette as they often did in the early afternoon after lunch was out of the way, and before they both went their separate ways for the afternoon, before dinner preparations began in earnest around four p.m.

"Get much?" Hattie asked.

"Five big ones! See what I'm making while you're just sitting around?"

"Whataya mean? We were just figuring out how we were gonna roll Miss Julie some dark night when she's out on one of her nature hikes? Did ya know she climbs trees?"

"No, I just met her, Hattie, and that ability doesn't always show up on first meetings."

"Well, your innocent eyeballs will be opened more clearly by tomorrow, no doubt. First, she does her breathing exercises out on the front lawn for all the world to see. Then, she's off to the pool down the street for twenty-five laps; and she doesn't drive there; she tip-toes! With a towel over her head so the sun won't crack her face-lift. Then, she tip-toes back here for breakfast, always late and always with nutty demands, like no spices, no poisons. She doesn't want anything that's good to eat or tastes good. Then she washes her undies in the back porch sink, brushing her teeth at the same time. In the afternoon, she does yoga exercises followed by a nap; and just before supper, off she goes again to the pool for more laps. Of course, like everything else, she's late for dinner. For about an hour beforehand, she races around upstairs nude from the bath to her room. I suggest if you really want an education, An-day, go upstairs about five-thirty and be on the lookout. She's got a good body for a dame her age, but she's got nothing else to do except take care of it."

"Errr . . . she always pays her bill in advance," said Miss Meyer. "So I don't care if she stands around nude in the front hall."

"Oh, now, Miss Meyer, you *know* you would," said Hattie.

It was true what Hattie said about Mrs. Lawson and her daily routine. She was out on the front lawn early the next morning clad in a white playsuit and sneakers, holding an umbrella over her head, doing her breathing exercises.

Right after breakfast, Mr. Lyon, who was with the French embassy in Washington, came bursting into the kitchen, dramatically demanding from Miss Meyer in a very loud voice, "Who ees theese woman geemnast?"

"Errr . . . it's Mrs. Lawson, Mr. Lyon. Is she bothering you?"

"No. Not at all. I'm rather enchanté by her performances. I want to talk weeth her."

"That should be cute," Hattie said afterwards. "He'll find out how enchante she is right after she checks his cavities."

All that day Caroline Cole, the chambermaid, and I watched Mrs. Lawson. While she washed her underwear on the back porch, she would be cleaning her teeth with some rubbery substance she chewed furiously in her mouth, twisting and contorting her face as she did so.

After she finished scrubbing her undies, she bent over the balcony above the clothesline and tossed her foundation garments to the lines, not bothering to go down and around and hang them up with pins. Sometimes her clothes hit the lines, and sometimes not; and if the wind from off the water were strong enough, some days, her things would be blown into the hedges and bushes.

One morning the milkman came into the kitchen with a grin on his face and carrying some of Mrs. Lawson's underwear with his milk. He looked at me and Mrs. Spurling, the pastry cook, and said, "Must have been quite a party here last night. I found these panties in the bushes halfway up the driveway!"

In the evenings, Mrs. Lawson would enter the dining room late, dramatically pausing in the entranceway, before going to her table. She was always attired in one of her 1948 get-ups, usually wrinkled and unironed, rips in her hose, and the straps of her high heel shoes undone. She'd often have flowers in her white-gloved hands for which she would request a vase.

"Flowers must always accompany me," she'd say, "even if just a bunch of ragweed." And the flowers, she ordered, were to stay on her dining room table or bedroom dresser until she herself threw them away, which meant never. Hattie, Caroline, or Miss Meyer would usually wait until the old flowers had become as crisp and brown as toast and then throw them out.

Anyway, Julie would pause in the dining room entranceway, looking quite lovely with her hair pulled back and her skin deeply tanned. She'd tip-toe across the room, greeting the other diners with her funny, little eccentric smile, and assume her position at her corner table. One's position in the dining room was determined by the time one stayed at the hotel. Since Mrs. Lawson outstayed everyone, and came early, she had the choice seat all season from which she had a full view of the ocean and Mount Desert Hills and also of the whole dining room.

As soon as she sat down, Hattie would announce to the kitchen staff, "Bring on the wheat germ and alligator milk! Scarlett O'Hara's ready to be served!"

Julie Lawson had let us all know that she wished no spices in her soup or food, no white bread, no ice cubes, no gravy, no rare meat, no rich desserts. She loved fresh fruit and wheat germ. She always had milk with her meals, no coffee. She had Kellogg's Concentrate sprinkled on top of everything.

After dinner, she walked around "the oval," as she called the Neck, and after that, she sat alone by herself, reading. She'd curl up on a couch or chair with her pumps off and peruse a book, but she'd hardly ever finish one. It became one of my daily duties to go about the house and grounds and pick up all of her unfinished books and put them back on the shelves. She took copious, hard-to-decipher notes on her readings and left them stuffed inside the books. I removed them and left them stacked on her bedroom dresser.

At the end of July, Mrs. Lawson spent a weekend away from the Manor down the coast at a boys' camp where her teenage son, her sole offspring, Parker Lawson III, spent the better part of his growing-up summers.

At the end of August, and her stay, Parker joined his mother at the Manor for a week or so. He was a tall, handsome, sandy-haired, blue-eyed fellow, as athletically inclined as his mother. He went swimming, exercising, running, and walking with her. He lifted weights and did not tip-toe. She measured his biceps regularly and they climbed trees together; they were frequently closeted in the bathroom giggling together. It was like Jane and Boy without Tarzan.

While Parker was around Mrs. Lawson was always radiantly happy; he was obviously the love of her life. Daily, she left him notes on their dining room table, under his door, by his bed. She made lists of books for him to read and rules for him to follow.

She clipped dozens of magazine articles for him to read while meals were being served. She was constantly intent on every facet of his education. And mostly he obeyed her; but I remember one evening, when Mother wasn't around, when Parker invited me up after work to his room for a talk. His room, like his mother's, was a mess with piles of underwear and socks in one corner, a stack of books and magazines in another, things scattered all over, the bed clothes rumpled. He offered me a drink; I could have grape-flavored Zarex or a Budweiser, both discouraged by his mother. He also showed me his suitcase collection of comic books and sex magazines. We sat there for a time ogling the girlies and sipping our Buds, Parker informing me what a cultured man should be looking for in a woman.

"I attend military school, like my father did," he told me. "I will try for West Point or the Citadel in two years."

"You really like the Army, huh?"

"I have an obligation. The Lawsons have always been Army men."

He didn't speak with me the way he did with his mother and the other guests. With me it was strictly man to boy. He lectured me, told me what life was all about. He assumed the military man-of-the-world stance, as my superior in all things. And I let him, because to my mind then, he *was* superior. I was lucky to be in his presence, to be considered good enough for him to spend time with. He was handsome and his body, with all that daily exercise and milk-drinking, was very muscular and tanned. He wore jeans, t-shirts, and sneakers like I did; yet he looked healthier, more capable, more ready and assured. He puzzled and intrigued me the whole time. He was so close with his mother, and yet he could be so tough. He drew a sharp line between the World of Men and his private existence. I thought then that a person who changed his behavior as radically as Parker did that evening with me had to have psychological problems, but I didn't tell him that. He did most of the talking anyway, and the talk centered around his great respect for his father and his father's supposed military exploits.

"Why doesn't your father come up here in the summers with you and your mother?"

"He was here once, but he doesn't share mother's appreciation for Maine or any other northern climate."

"How come?" I asked, not accustomed to hearing of someone disliking my native land.

"He's a southerner. The farthest he will go north is Washington where he visits the Senate. He took me to the Senate with him last year."

"Is he in politics?"

"All rich men are in politics. They have to protect their money."

And so it went. The next day I told Hattie about my evening as Parker's guest.

"What a little jerk that poor boy is," she said.

"Jerk! He's rich and smart."

"He's queer like his mother. Haven't you heard 'em giggling together? He'll never break away from her. She won't let him."

"But he admires his father a lot."

"His father is a handsome snob. He came up here a few summers ago and strutted around like he was reviewing the troops. I could go for him physically, but he was crazy, too, like the whole lot of 'em. Julie herself says that he married her for her money. The Lawsons were broke and he didn't want or know how to work, so he married her and can sit around in his Army uniform on his veranda down in Tampa, sipping his mint julep. He thinks he's still commanding over in Europe like he did in the War. There's no love there; she says so. All her love goes to Parker and that's the boy's problem. She'll never let him grow up on his own. He'll be queer; you'll see."

"He drinks beer and reads girlie magazines," I noted.

"Thank God for that much. The poor boy's trying, but it's a lost cause, I'm afraid. He pretends, but he's in need of a lot of help."

I really didn't see what she meant, for I was blinded by Parker's dashing appearance and by my own unworldliness. I really thought looks and money like he had were enough. If he were queer, as Hattie said, then I wanted to be queer like that.

That last day, the Lawsons started leaving early in the morning but didn't actually pull out of the back parking lot until mid-afternoon. Things were re-packed the way they came, wherever they fit.

"We drive to Portland," Julie told us, the entire staff assembled there for the occasion. "Tomorrow, we pick up Eric, a college boy who drives us to New York and Tampa. I hope the trek won't prove too ravaging . . . Parker and I wish you all . . ."

She never finished what she was wishing us. Typical of Mrs. Lawson.

"Look, Julie, you and Parker drive carefully. We'll see you next summer," said Hattie.

"Ummm," hummed Julie, smiling that funny little smile.

Driving out, she managed to take only half of the cedar hedge with her.

"I'm glad to see Julie really listened to my advice." said Hattie.

THE LOBSTER STOMP

ONE SATURDAY NIGHT, over twenty years ago, when I was working as a kitchen boy down at Frenchman's Bay Manor, a now defunct summer hotel on exclusive Red Cliff Neck, Hattie Pinkham, the head waitress, asked me to go to The Lobster Stomp with her and Glory, her married daughter. Since I hadn't been to a dance all that summer, I agreed to the proposition. We drove in Hattie's old '52 Plymouth sedan nicknamed Lulabelle up Route One to West Hamlin to the old Sorosis Hall which had been generously rebuilt and refurbished by one of the benevolent summer folk, a doctor, I believe, who had entertained some noble vision about founding a cultural center for the area which would incorporate a library, a woman's club, a youth organization, a place for year-round concerts, lectures, parties, art exhibits, and a host of other activities for the benefit of the surrounding communities. Translated, however, into Downeast practicality, the new center became as the old: a dance hall. And the Navy boys from the Bay Harbor base who frequented the place every Saturday night had christened the handsome new Recreation Center "The Lobster Stomp." The orchestra that was giving its concert that evening was a motley get-together of local musicians who called themselves "Pearly Allen and His All-Stars."

When we arrived, the joint was jumping, out in the parking lot as much as in the hall. And what a strange mixture of people was present. Along the sidelines, seated on the folding chairs, milling about the kitchen area, hanging around the front hall were native Mainiacs and summer foreigners, local bums and Navy boys. They all stood ogling, watching, sipping their beverages, smoking, talking about and to each other, occasionally asking each other to dance.

Since this was a dry dance by law, the locals had to bring their booze in Canada Dry Ginger Ale or Pepsi bottles which they passed back and forth out of the light, grinning and giggling over their naughtiness.

As we entered the hall itself, Hattie turned to Glory and me and said, "I love to dance, so let's hope this week I can find another two-legged animal who can at least swing me around the floor without busting my kneecaps."

Blond and pony-tailed Glory, as amusingly tough as her mother, replied, "You sure are choosey, Ma. I'll be happy if I get someone who can stand up straight."

"What are you talking about?" asked Hattie. "Who wants to dance with a straight man?"

"You're the lucky one, An-day," Hattie said. "At least you get to ask."

"And get refused," I said.

I looked around, while Hattie and Glory went their separate ways amongst the crowd, to see if I could find anyone whom I knew. To my relief, there were several familiar faces, but they did not belong to close acquaintances.

There was this one creepy bespectacled fellow who had been in several of my classes at nearby Mollusk Memorial High School. He had on a baggy brown suit and held a Pepsi in his hand. He accosted me first at the edge of the floor. His name was Uriel Marin, and he was known about school as a very odd character, hung up on religion.

"I'm not supposed to be here, ya know," he told me, his eyeballs nearly bulging out of his head.

"No, I wasn't aware of that, Uriel; why not?" I asked, trying to sound bored, to get him away from me. All I needed was to be identified with this freak to be ostracized for the entire evening.

"I'm a hard-shell Baptist," he said. "We're not supposed to play cards, go to the movies, or dance or drink. I'm sinning tonight!"

"Then why did you come?"

"Because I'm weak, just like my foster mother said."

"Then you don't really believe in your religion."

"Oh, yes! I do! I'm a very strong believer, and I know right now that I'm standing in a house of sin with sinners all about me. And I'm sinning! I would not complain if we were all to be wiped out this instant by God, because this is a wicked, evil place!" Uriel took a swig from his Pepsi bottle.

"Is your Pepsi spiked, Uriel?"

"Of course not!" he said. "But even without the taint of liquor, it's still a strong, filthy stimulant not fit for human consumption!"

"Then why in hell are ya swilling it?"

"I told ya! I'm very weak. I have relapses unless I have constant guidance."

"Have you danced, Uriel?" I asked. "I think it's fun."

"Well, you're an infidel to begin with and don't know your head from a hole in the ground! You're in the dark!"

"All the better for dancing."

As the All Stars were playing an unreasonable facsimile of "The World Is Waiting for the Sunrise," Hattie swung by me in the arms of some old gray-haired codger, looking very young, pretty, and gay, calling to me, "An-day! Give one of those girls on the sidelines a chance!"

Glory, like her mother, was dancing with a man I hardly considered her equal. How could really smart women like them let such men buy their affections? Did they want to dance that much? Glory's partner, for instance, was a local sometime-lobsterman who always had a stubble of beard on his face, and who always wore cheap cotton work clothes, even to a Saturday night dance. But Glory seemed, like her mother, to be making the best of it, and giving him a good time. Perhaps I shouldn't be so bothered by it all, I thought.

But I didn't want to dance with just anyone. I wanted to have the guts to ask one of the summer girls. There was this one in particular that evening, a pretty, well-tanned, brown-haired girl who had on a white party dress and who sat against the wall with another pretty blonde and an older, handsome man who looked as if he might be their father. They had class, I could tell. The way they looked; they seemed amused in their slumming experience. I reasoned that people like them couldn't have come to the Lobster Stomp for reasons other than curiosity. It would be fun to go home and tell about this hick joint. For awhile, I sat near them. The brown-haired girl was one of the prettiest girls I had ever seen and I loved the way she laughed, talked, and moved.

To my shock and disgust, Wendell West, one of my classmates who affected one of the then current Downeast imitations of Elvis Presley, asked Miss Brown Hair to dance, and she accepted! Wendell was good-looking and muscular in a greasy sort of way. He had on his usual tight Levis which he wore beltless and low on his hips, and he had on a silky, bright-colored shirt open to the waist, and no undershirt so that everyone could see his chest. His long black hair was combed into a well-oiled D.A. and hung in his face. The girls at school had labeled him arrogant, cheap, rough, and over-sexed;

and as far as I knew, not one of them had ever refused an invitation to date him. When Wendell danced, even with this classy summer girl, he struggled as close as he could without suffocating his partner; it was obvious that Wendell considered his dance only a prelude to the main event in the parking lot.

In my nice boy's delusion, I just couldn't understand why Hattie, Glory, and Miss Brown Hair would dance and keep on dancing with this inferior type of male person. Couldn't they see, as I thought I did, that they wouldn't amount to anything?

Perley's All Star Band was hopelessly outmoded and behind the times. They didn't play any rock-'n-roll. Their repertoire consisted mostly of variations on "Blue Moon," "Stardust," and for a fast beat, "The Beer Barrel Polka." They did play a couple of Virginia Reels, one of which I danced with Gracie Ray, a buxom, middle-aged bleached blonde woman from my hometown of Taunton who was always dressed as a cowgirl with fringe on her sleeves and skirts and with fancy high-heeled boots. Every Fourth of July, Gracie led the Bay Harbor parade down Cottage Street astride her proudest possession, her golden palomino horse. She was a great and lovely character with her teased blonde hair, her dangling earrings, and her raspy voice. Dancing a reel with her was one of the two good moments for me in the evening.

The other moment came when I danced with Linda Terrapin, a pretty, tall, long-haired girl, who was a year behind me in school, an intelligent girl who came originally from out-of-state. She was very witty, an excellent science student (her homemade tarpaper telescope had won her a prize in the preceding year's county science fair at Ellsworth), and she liked me. We danced several dances and I bought her several cokes. We sat for quite awhile talking and making each other laugh on the sidelines. I imitated some of the summer people in deriding my local neighbors, poking fun at their antics, laughing at this or that "character," like Uriel.

The worst moment for me in the evening came when I asked this other girl to dance. She had been a freshman at Mollusk, two years behind me, and was cute. I thought she'd be very glad to dance with a prominent junior honors student like me, but she refused! I felt humiliated and angry, and didn't understand how such a dumb little bitch like her could refuse me, not only one of the school's best students, but a member of our state champion cross country team and soon to be college man at the University of Maine. My confidence had increased after the time spent with Linda, who was much prettier than this freshman, so I was really crestfallen and confused by this refusal from someone so obviously inferior to me. I thought I was doing the little freshman a favor.

On the way back to Bay Harbor that night, Hattie and Glory made me feel better with their constant joking. When we pulled into the yard of Glory's house, every light in the house was on, and her lobsterman husband was drunk and waiting for her in the doorway.

"Oh, gawd," she said, when she saw him. "He must have his dander up."

"That might be exciting," said Hattie.

"Are you kidding?" Glory asked, as she got out of the car. "Good night, Mama. Good night, An-day. See ya later."

"I hope so, Glor-ay," I said.

"Where the hell have you been?" shouted her silhouetted and shirtless husband from the house as she walked towards him.

"Oh, shut up! I've been out with mama!"

"Jesus H. Christ! This is a fine goddamn thing! Git in here where ya belong before I kick your ass!"

"Had enough to drink?" Glory asked to his face, standing up to him on the doorstep, finally shoving him inside with one hand and closing the door behind them with her other.

Hattie began to back Lulabelle out of the driveway when I asked her, "Will Glor-ay be all right, Hattie?"

"Hell, yes. Don't worry about them. That's the way they make love."

COCKTAILS ON THE POINT

IT HAD BEEN A PERFECT AUGUST DAY on the coast of Maine, one of those few late summer days with no fog or even any haze. The waters of Frenchman's Bay sparkled brilliantly in the sunlight, the leaves of the deciduous trees stirred ever so sensuously in the slight warm breeze. Many summer folk had gone a-sailing. A few crossbills had been spotted on the West Side of Taunton Point; and the annual tennis tournament was in full swing.

I was at the library, where I'd assumed the post as summer librarian for the past few summers; and where, because of the glorious weather, only a handful of people had been all day. It was near closing time, which is five p.m., and I did want to close a bit early since I was invited to a cocktail party at Marietta Clemson's. Towards the end of summer, there seemed to be such a party practically every night of the week at someone's cottage; and even though the cast of guests hardly ever varied from this porch to that living room, the food and drink were free and the conversation, while not always as sparkling as the waters of Frenchman's Bay, could often be engrossing. After all, most of the summer people were educated and well-read, world travelers who usually had something perceptive or witty to say on most issues, whether of local or national and international interest. Former ambassadors, government officials, professors, doctors, lawyers, businessmen, artists, experts in one field or another — they had all done a great deal with their lives;

and most of them were well worth listening to. Even though many of them were retired, they still kept up with what was going on in the world. It was great fun for me to serve as librarian to such a clientele.

But before I could leave work for the latest round of drinks, goodies, and bon mots, I had to pick up around the bibliotheque, turn off the Mr. Coffee machine, make sure all the doors and windows were closed and locked, all the faucets upstairs and down were turned off, and get rid of my final customer of the day, who for the past hour had been Roman Garcia, a handsome, serious young man of Spanish origin, who had just graduated from a Maine prep school and was planning on studying architecture at Cornell in the fall. He had been looking at new books we had on Irish castles and Maine's shingle-style summer cottages in the "Fran Collingsworth Room," a reading room named for a former prominent summer lady and classicist who had literally been knocked out of her sneakers on the Point road years before by a hit-and-run driver.

Attired in the typical American teenage male's outfit of faded Levis, t-shirt, and Adidas sneakers, Roman was bent over the architecture books at a small table in the reading room when I came in to tell him that I'd like to close early.

"Oh, sure," he said, starting to get up right away. And as he handed me both books to take out, he asked, "A lot of the houses here on The Point are shingle-style, aren't they?" Roman had recently moved to Taunton with his mother, who was Spanish, and his American step-father.

"Yes, I'm headed for one of them right now," I said, in reference to Mrs. Clemson's twenty room cottage overlooking Frenchman's Bay.

"Why were they all built of unpainted cedar shingles?"

"Probably the shingles were cheap and plentiful then; and also they give that nice, gray weathered look. Such structures blend in more with the haunting scenery around here. 'Plain living and high thinking,' ya know; that was their motto—the founders of this place."

"Was it? That's funny," said Roman, his well-tanned, handsome young face lighting up with a smile. The summer before he had had an affair, which had delighted The Point, with the beautiful, young, statuesque daughter of a prominent long-time Point family. Everyone on The Point with a heart took an interest in the affair.

"That's what their descendants like to claim," I said, "but I'm not sure as to the truth of either part of the phrase. Certainly, one couldn't say there was all that much high thinking going on today by the titles of the books that go out of this place the most. These two tomes you're checking out are the heaviest I've seen all week.

Mostly, it's Sidney Sheldon, Judith Krantz, Stephen King, James Michener — all the best sellers and the latest mysteries."

"But there are some very good books in here," said Roman.

"Oh, yes, but they move slowly these days. People don't come for all summer any more; and if they are here just for a week or two, they only want light reading."

"I wish there were a few more books on architecture."

"Maybe I'll be able to get you some more before the summer ends. We can do Interlibrary Loans, ya know. And I'll inform the trustees."

"Thank you. Well, see you later." He started to walk toward the front door.

"Roman, I can give you a ride, unless you want to walk. I'm going right by your place."

"O.K.; where are you going for drinks?"

"Marietta Clemson's."

"Oh!" he said with a knowing laugh. "Marietta! Isn't she the character!"

"Yes, I'd say she certainly was."

"She's also very blunt with her opinions."

"That she is."

Being home down on The Point again after being away from Maine teaching in New York was strange. The place hadn't changed much, except for a few new houses here and there. How well I remembered most of the old places, since I had helped open them and close them all of my growing up summers. I had washed their windows, scrubbed their toilets, swept their floors, mowed their lawns, and delivered the milk from my grandfather's farm to their kitchens. My mother and most of my aunts cleaned the cottages and worked as cooks and did the laundries; and had done so all of their lives. My father and many of my uncles and other male relatives worked as caretakers and handymen servicing the summer places. Next to working at one of the town's two lobster pounds, or in the woods, or on the Maine Central Railroad, the summer colony was, for many of the town's families, something one could always count on at least for part-time work during the summer months, like worming or clamming.

I was really quite anxious to see everyone over drinks because this was the first party I had been invited to since my five-part radio series entitled "The Maine That's Missing," based on a previous article of mine in *Maine Life*, had been broadcast over the Maine Public Broadcasting System. I knew that some of the Point people had been tuned in and I was naturally anxious to learn of their reactions.

As I walked in the front door of the Clemson cottage, Marietta herself greeted me by saying, "I must take umbrage!"

"Must you, Marietta? Where shall we take it?"

"No further than this foyer. I just wanted to warn you that some people thought your radio series was very poorly edited and that the whole thing amounted to Andy Griffin's ego trip."

"Thanks, Marietta. That really makes me feel good. Maybe I should just turn around and go back to the library?"

"Oh, no! We need you here to spark a little controversy. I was just warning you. I don't think anyone's going to bite your head off. Maybe no one will even mention it. Proceed out to the porch. It's a simply glorious day and the booze and food are all over the tables out there. Go help yourself."

"Thanks."

Out on the great porch which ran the length of Marietta's large cottage and from which one faced a magnificent view of the bay and the Mount Desert Hills and Island several miles across, I fixed myself a good-sized Scotch and soda and began to meander about among the guests, running first of all into Ambrose LaGrange, a portly raconteur and recently retired classics professor from the University of Virginia, who greeted me by saying, "Well, here comes the uppity native!"

"That's good, Ambrose. I like that label."

"Well, I'd say after this summer that it's a rather apt cognomen, wouldn't you?"

"You are referring to my series, 'The Maine That's Missing'?"

"What else? Now, what in hell do you mean by 'The Maine That's Missing'? *My* Maine isn't missing. It's right here, same as always. Hasn't changed much since I was a tadpole."

"Of course not. Your Maine is the summer folks' Maine and that must be preserved at all costs. But what I was primarily getting at in both the original article in *Maine Life* and on the series is that there's precious little available in print, the commercial media, or in advertising that I've ever seen about 'my Maine,' the native's Downeast as I've known it growing up here in Hancock County."

"But who wants to read that sort of stuff? Of course, we know it goes on, here and everywhere else; but we come to Maine in the summers to be renewed and refreshed by the natural surroundings. We don't want to read about the local *Tobacco Road* sin scene."

"Now, that's certainly an insult. I don't think my parents or relatives or neighbors are fresh out of *Tobacco Road.*"

"Well, maybe not your relatives; but certainly up the road from here there are a number of shacks with overturned cars in the yard."

"That's what I'm talking about. Maine is not all gracious summer cottages with noble lobstermen on every pier. There's a dark side that either gets glossed over or totally left out or over-romanticized."

"Well, yes, but Maine *is* romantic. It has an image to keep up just like Texas does and New York and Key West. People need their romantic myths, Andy. Keeps us going."

"And keeps the tourists coming."

"Of course. Maine must keep up appearances. That's what most people are here for — appearances. No one wants to spend vacation money in Bar Harbor to learn about the seedy goings-on among the wormdiggers, just as you don't want to go to New York to get mugged."

As I talked at length with Ambrose, I was reminded of my very first cocktail party on Taunton Point, which had occurred the first summer I became librarian. The invitation had come from one of the newest families to arrive on The Point. At that party, I had met a New York banker whose family had summered in Maine for generations. A few months previous, I had had my one and only article on worm-digging in Maine published in the New York *Times*, and the banker began his association with me by asking me *how* I got the article in the *Times.* "I'm a good writer," I said; but not wishing to be too sarcastic, I hastily explained how a *Times* financial editor, and my friend, had the idea of running a series of articles on people around the country who had made money, like former President Carter had, in relatively offbeat occupations such as peanut farming or worm-digging.

And here I sat on The Point trying to explain myself once again.

"Don't you think it's strange, Ambrose, that I'll probably be the only local yokel here today at this gathering? The only Maine native?"

"No, because you're our librarian. We have that in common with you; and also because you're uppity. Good God, we can't take too much more of this liberation stuff. The blacks, the Chicanos, the homosexuals, the feminists; and now, the Maine natives! Everyone's in revolt! It gets a bit tiresome. I haven't been cruel to you Maine natives. I've paid for my cottage; and I've paid for services; and every year the taxes go up, but I'm not complaining. I love it here and I expect to pay the going rate for summering in Maine with a view of Bar Harbor. But I'll be goddamned if I'm going to invite all of your worm-digging relatives in for a drink. However, I'll invite *you* in because I know you and I like you and we have things we can talk about. If you're so upset about the lack of 'real Maine stories about real Maine folk,' then, the way I see it, you're going to have to write them yourself."

"Maybe you're right."

"Well, of course, I am! I'm a well-educated summer person."

"You do drive a Mercedes."

"That's my wife's! And it's ten years old!"

Joining us at about this point was Karen Madison, one of the best-liked hostesses on Taunton Point. She sat down next to me, with her drink, and touched my arm. She was well-tanned and dressed in a pretty white outfit.

"Andy, I just wanted to tell you that I only caught a bit of one of your programs, but I was greatly interested in the whole project."

"Thank you, Karen. I wish I had interviewed you for it."

"Yes, I could have told the story of the ultra-snobby summer lady, *not* a resident of Taunton Point, who came up to me once at a party and asked, 'Do you live here year-round?' 'Yes,' I said. 'How do you cope with the problem of mingling with the natives?' 'Well, you see, for me that's no problem. I *am* a native!' "

"Now you see," interrupted Ambrose, "how you were wrong, Andy. There is another native here. You forgot Karen."

"Yes, I did."

"It's sometimes difficult to know who's assimilated," he said. "You know, Karen, Andy is getting just like the Maine Indians. Soon he'll want his ancestral hunting lands back!"

Marietta interrupted all of us to announce, "How many of you will be sampling our simply marvelous homemade orange and lemon sherbet? It's a secret recipe and ever so tangy!"

"Marietta," said Karen, "I tried to get you last night but I couldn't."

"No, I was in Bangor picking up a grandchild from the airport and then I took her to the Polynesian Restaurant where she had supper and I had a martini and an eggroll."

"Oh, how is it there now? I haven't been there in ages."

"It's fine if you want a martini and an eggroll. I don't know about all that incomprehensible stuff that comes to you in the dark. Now, how many for sherbet?"

Karen declined, but Ambrose and I said we'd try some.

As the afternoon became evening, and the lights from across the bay began to twinkle, I talked with a dozen more people, most of whom mentioned the radio series.

One lady professor said she had had a house guest from NBC who said the one program they heard was poorly edited.

"I hope you informed her that the Maine Public Broadcasting System does not have the resources and staff, as yet, of NBC," I said. "It was a two-man operation with over sixty interviews."

And then there was the New York socialite who asked me how I could say such awful things about E. B. White. "Comparing him with Grace Metalious and *Peyton Place*! That was just dreadful! E. B. White is why I came here, you know."

"Personal invitation?"

"Oh, no. I've never met him in person; but I used to lie in my berth on our boat right off here in the bay and read E. B. White's wonderful essays about this part of Maine; and I just knew that some day I'd be here; but I was outraged to hear over the radio how you said he wasn't truly Maine!"

"I didn't say that. One of the Maine people who was interviewed said that what Grace Metalious had written in *Peyton Place* was truer to his Maine than the lovely essays of Mr. White, whom all of us admire, of course, as a writer."

"Well, what is this *true Maine*? How is it different from what E. B. White writes?"

"I guess you'd have to grow up here, go to school here, work and live here year-round for many years to see what I was driving at."

Cocktails on The Point traditionally lasted for about two hours, and just before seven that particular night, I got into an extended conversation with Vera Anderson, one of the most respected women on Taunton Point, a lifelong resident; and her reaction to "The Maine That's Missing" was to tell me a story from her youth.

"As an idealistic student at Vassar in the 1920's, I naturally wanted to pitch in and help change the world for the better. As you know, my parents, my brother, sister, and I all used to come here to The Point, every summer, for the whole summer; we'd play tennis, go on hikes, sailing, picnics; and it was just wonderful. The best summers you can imagine. My father was a professor, and so were many of the other people here; and they spent their summers reading, writing, doing research, working on important projects. And so when I got the opportunity to stay on here to work one winter with Miss Beazley, a Maine minister, probably the first woman minister with the Sea Coast Mission, I jumped at the chance. I thought it would be just great to assist her in her work with all the Maine people out on the islands and along the coast. She married people, baptized them, buried them; and there was even a daily Bible school for which I had to prepare three prayers a week. I never worked so hard in my life: scrubbing floors, washing clothes, ironing, chopping wood, hauling water, cooking, playing the organ, and even preaching! I was her slave. She was big, red-haired, and almost devoid, as I learned later, of any real Christian charity; but she was a great character and I had wonderful and awful experiences with her. We'd go on the boat with Brother Miller to what seemed like dozens of islands. I remember the first little Maine girl that I asked, 'Dear, do you say your prayers before you go to bed?' And she replied, 'Hell, no! Daddy pees and then we all get into bed together!' At one of the testimonial meetings I attended on one of the islands, I remember this woman standing up and saying, 'I wish I had the wings of a dove that I might fly to the arms of my Savior!' And right after she said that, an old man popped right up, and hollared, 'Sit down, ya old fool! Ya'd get shot for a crow 'fore ya got there!' Some of the living conditions shocked me, like the case of one woman who lived with three men and all her children in the same shack, and I don't believe anyone really listened to all of our good Christian advice; but these were good people for the most part, and I loved them. But I never knew much about Maine people, or Maine, until that year I spent here. I learned that Maine people, for instance, are far from laconic. I used to hook rugs with the women, and I'd never heard such God-awful chit-chat. They talked endlessly. And I also learned that many of them were awfully mean, but it was a mean, hard place to live. At the meetings with Miss Beazley, we'd all have to recite a Bible verse every time, and I was always amazed at how all the lobstermen had a verse to say. One of my favorites, and still is, was 'I will lift up mine eyes unto the hills.' I think about that line every day that I'm here gazing across the bay to Mount Desert. Oh, Andy, this wonderful place has changed the least of all the places in my life in the last fifty years; and that's why I still love it so. We've all sold our houses in other places, but none of us here would ever sell our Maine cottages. You know, a good many of the summer people here have had their ashes scattered over Frenchman's Bay; and that's where I plan to have mine scattered."

"Who's scattering ashes?" asked Marietta coming towards Vera and me to say goodnight. "Not on my rug, I hope!"

"I was just telling Andy how I wanted mine scattered over the bay," said Vera.

"Well, of course," said Marietta. "We certainly don't want to be buried up at the local cemetery with all those Maine natives!"

THE RETURNED NATIVE

THE THREE WARREN SISTERS were in Sid's kitchen, Bunny and Pill sitting at the table talking with Sid who was cutting out a blouse.

"I wish they'd get some better bras over to Ellsworth," said Sid.

"Yes, aren't those ones into Zayre's and Woolco's flimsy!" said Bunny.

"That's the type the gals wear nowadays," said Pill. "They show everything you've got."

"A good many of today's gals don't wear any at all," said Sid.

"I wish I could manufacture 'em," said Bunny. "Remember how Alna, who was real busty, used to just tie a towel around her for a bra?"

"Yes," said Pill, "it seems to me she did do that. She used to always make fun of you because you weren't as ample as she was."

"Don't I know it!" said Bunny. "I miss Alna. She was always a lot of fun. You could always drop in and see her and she'd have a funny story or two. And when we were little kids, a couple of centuries ago, she used to signal with a white pillowcase from her house down the field for Pill and me to come down and play. I grew up with a little pindly body with a big head and my legs doubled right under me. I used to crouch under the kitchen table chewing toilet paper, but since them days I've been a tough old bird."

"At least you had a neck," said Pill. "I've had to go through life with no neck and looking like Mamie Eisenhower!"

"You know who I saw recently stumbling around Main Street over to Ellsworth?" asked Bunny.

"Who?" asked Sid.

"Glad-Ass. Remember her? I'm surprised she's still kicking. We used to play with her when we were all kids. She was a state girl and used to yell at us, 'You Warrens think you're so smart because your father was a schoolteacher, but you're all black!' "

"Who did she marry?" asked Sid.

"She married one of the Bradford twins over in North Hamlin," said Pill.

"Yes, they say she used to take turns with the twins on the kitchen floor so one of 'em had to marry her," said Bunny.

"They always said she was mentally bad, but, by God, she could produce children," said Pill.

"Had a dozen or more, didn't she?" asked Sid.

"I think it was fourteen that lived," said Bunny. "She helped populate Hancock County; but what used to tickle me — even her own kids called her Glad-Ass."

"She became an awful drunk after her last husband died," said Pill. "Used to have a bottle of whiskey every night."

"That's why I was surprised to see her still alive," said Bunny.

"Some of her kids turned out real nice. That Beecher who used to drive the Harris Bakery truck was one of her boys," said Sid.

"Yes," said Bunny, "and there's that fancy guy who lives down on the Crooked Road. They call him Nimmy. He lives with that big fat, red-headed woman; but he's a real dandy. What they call a gay boy nowadays. He'll never hurt her. She's his friend."

"Anyway, Glad-Ass certainly is a character," said Pill.

"And speaking of characters," said Sid, "I got a call last night that Lillie's coming home either this July or August."

"That sounds just like Lil," said Bunny. "Real definite plans."

"She'll be up doing her laundry and hair in the middle of the night," said Bunny.

"No, I don't think so," said Sid. "She's been getting better with every visit. The last time home she only had three suitcases, her guitar, and stereo system with her. She did leave me with a terrific phone bill, however."

"Lillie has her own little style," said Pill.

"What got me that last time after she left here," said Bunny, "she stopped off in Seattle to have her nose fixed before going back to Alaska."

"When we get the final word," said Sid, "we'll have to save at least two days to have to go to the Bangor Airport and meet all the planes. She always has a foul-up, ya know. And we have to get ourselves all scrubbed up for a week because she ties up the bathroom; and we have to dig out the lard pails for her to go blueberrying with."

It's true that my cousin Lillie's infrequent visits over the past fourteen years, since she had been working and living in Alaska, were always a bit bothersome for everyone in the family; but they were also major social events that everyone talked about afterwards for months. When Lil was in residence, everyone dropped by to see her. After all, she had always been one of the stars of our family. Her picture, the only one from among the thirty-five Warren grandchildren, hung on the wall in our grandparents' house. Beautiful and lively, with jet black hair and big brown eyes, Lillie had always been a "bewitching little thing." Smart, too. Valedictorian of her grammar school, high school, and junior college classes, Lil had garnered more than her share of academic honors. She had been chosen a DAR Good Citizen in high school, won several scholarships and prizes, including Miss Lobster Boat, and ultimately graduated magna cum laude from Brandeis University. "Not bad for a little Christian gal in the big Jewish school," said Lil at the time; and we couldn't help but agree. But we weren't all that surprised either. We always expected her to get all A's.

In high school, Lillie was elected "best-looking," "most active in school affairs," and "most likely to succeed." She was a cheerleader, she was in the band, she acted in plays, and she got to go out with the best-looking and most popular boys. Even as a freshman, she got to date seniors and boys from the Navy base. She was a good dancer and a teacher's pet. Many other girls naturally felt envious. However, she was never particularly good at organized sports. She loved music and the theater; but she also wanted to be a medical doctor. Her elaborate, life-sized re-creations in cardboard of the body's respiratory and cardio-vascular systems won her a first prize at the Hancock County Science Fair; and when we were kids, playing together up in the shed chamber of our house, while I had my TV studio, Lillie had her hospital made out of cardboard boxes and orange crates. She even had fashioned medical instruments out of aluminum foil. After high school, rejecting a bid from Mount Holyoke, Lillie went instead to Boston to the Carnegie School of Medical Technology. Except for one miserable year at the University of Maine at Orono, Lillie spent the seven years after high school in the Boston area, going to school (ultimately to three of them), and working as a medical technologist.

Growing up together in Taunton Ferry, Lil and I enjoyed a comparatively free-wheeling, imaginative, and creative companionship. We romped and played along the shore, went swimming in the salt water, hiking and blueberrying through the fields and woods. We built tree houses, started a secret club, collected beach glass and sea shells, and went flounder fishing at the lobster pound. Since we lived next door to each other, we saw each other every day. We both loved books, music, and the movies; took piano lessons together; and headed up our Congregational Church youth group. Since we were first cousins, our mothers were always afraid we'd fall in love with each other; and, of course, we did. One hot summer day, just before the onset of puberty, Lillie and I went swimming nude down to the shore, only to be severely chastised by my mother, Sid, who suddenly appeared up on the bank in my father's old green 1950 Chevy pickup. She screamed at us to get out of the water and put our clothes back on; and as we scrambled dutifully up the bank, she pulled an alder switch from the clump growing there to beat me with. Naturally, to Sid's eyes, such a scene had to be the boy's fault. Boys were such nasty creatures, and I was a year older, after all.

With the onset of puberty, it seemed the most natural thing in the world for me to show off the muscles in my arms to my beloved Cousin Lillie, and so I was always chinning myself on tree limbs in front of her, and strutting around in my new tight jeans. And one cold November afternoon upstairs in my house when my parents were gone to a hunting camp, when Lil was twelve and I was thirteen or so, we took off our clothes again and revealed ourselves to each other. We laughed and laughed, as we always did when in each other's company.

But when I turned fourteen, our relationship changed. Until that time, we had never needed anyone else in our little world. We had always been together. Even when she was away with her family for a weekend visiting relatives in South Paris or Bangor, I knew she'd be back soon; and anytime I wanted to I could go down to her house and we would play records, read to each other for hours from favorite books, gossip, or play mad-libs, which we loved to make-up, or other word games. But one night, in her bedroom, she told me we couldn't play in the shed chamber any more. It was the time to put away childish things; and I was crushed. This first rejection from the person I loved most in my life hit me hard. For a while, I tried playing up in the shed chamber alone and making up mad-libs for myself; but it was hardly the same. Lillie was now spending her time with her girlfriends, going on dates, and going most places without me. After a while, she had her life and I had mine.

But why Alaska? That was something all of us couldn't figure out, since Lil had always hated the cold weather so while growing up in Maine. My only clue was the fact that she had loved an old technicolor movie called "The Wild North," starring Stewart Granger and Wendell Corey, when we were kids. She had made her parents take her to Ellsworth two or three times to see it. She even made her own paper cartoon version of it which she showed to me. And Lillie, despite the years in Boston, had never liked the big city. She had a definite animal streak to her which preferred and hungered for the wild outdoors. She loved to dash alone about the fields and woods and along the shores of Taunton. She'd often go out for long walks at twilight time, even at night, and during storms. At such times, with her long black hair blowing about her beautiful face, she reminded me of Catherine on the moors in *Wuthering Heights.*

Alaska had come after theatrical stints in Southern California and Hawaii, where Lillie had worked in various shows and where she had met a stunt man on a television series entitled appropriately enough "Mission Impossible." He had gone to Alaska to fight forest fires and she had gone after him. The affair was off and on again for years. Lillie came home for a year in the early 1970's to work as a medical technologist in Ellsworth, the same trade she kept at in Anchorage; but Alaska drew her back again. "Once you've lived there," she said, "you can't get it out of your system. It's like Maine."

And so in the summer of 1981, it turned out to be for two weeks in August, Lillie came home again, amidst the usual flurry of phone calls from airports across the country and this time an air controllers' strike to complicate things further. Finally, some time in the early evening, she called from Boston to say she'd be in Bangor in an hour or so, and with the usual mix-up, both Lillie's sister Lovina and I went in separate cars to pick her up.

While waiting for Lillie's plane to land, Lovina, at one point, said to me, "Ya know why Lil had her nose fixed in Seattle, don't ya?"

"No, not really. I never noticed anything wrong with her nose. She always looked great to me."

"She's so vain, and has always been bothered by her bowed legs all her life and now putting on more weight, that she decided to make her face perfect. Her nose was just a teensy bit crooked, so she had it fixed; that's what I think. She wanted a perfect face."

Whether that indeed was the case or not, the nose job, just like every other development in Lillie's life, didn't surprise me. Standing there that night, waiting for Lil, just as I have for so many days and nights, I could close my eyes and see her over the years.

At home, in Taunton, at the Congregational Church singing better and louder than anyone else in the choir. And in the same church on the same altar she and I singing "Frosty the Snowman" together as a Christmas duet.

We were always putting on shows. In grammar school, as a break between rock-'n-roll sessions before school started, Lillie and I would lip-sync many of Spike Jones' most famous routines. One night, thrill of thrills, Lillie with her friend Charlene, got to sing "Ricochet Romance" on the school stage with the Northern Lights, a young Downeast trio of country and western singers.

At high school, I remember Lillie singing "April Love" in her new purple dress from Robert Hall's in the school gym for the spring variety show.

And I could see her at the North Hamlin quarry in the summertime sunning herself in her bathing suit, with her girlfriends, trying to attract the Navy boys, who were diving off the cliffs.

All through school, going off on dates with a variety of young swains in their flashy new cars, driving by me while I was mowing the lawn.

Later, in Cambridge, with friends at Harvard, eating at a French restaurant at Harvard Square, trying out our school French.

In New York, in Greenwich Village, eating and drinking in an outdoors cafe in the pouring rain.

At home, standing in front of the door in the light from the porch-light, greeting me and Sid in tears with blood over the front of her dress. The blood was from her fiance who had been killed that morning on the way to Cape Cod in a motorcycle accident. She had been driving her MG behind him when he was hit by a truck. She had driven all the way home to Maine that night.

Upstairs in our house, in my brother's bedroom, crying with me on the bed after the funeral for Aunt Eller, Lillie's mother.

And always down on the shore I could picture her, gathering wrinkles at low tide, gathering pussy willows out in the woods, sailing on the bay and driving a speedboat out on the pond, ice skating in the winter, running through the summer fields of buttercups and daisies, laughing as we played endless games of Flinch, Monopoly, Clue, Gin Rummy, Dominoes, and Chinese Checkers.

And here she was again, waving to Lovina, Lovina's husband, their kids, and me from the line of people coming through the gate at Bangor International Airport. Still the same, except for a few gray strands in her long dark hair, still smiling her Miss Lobster Boat smile.

"Well, howdy!" she said in greeting. "The prodigal daughter —

and sister — returns. How in hell are ya? My dear hearts and gentle folk?"

Lots of hugs and kisses; and then on the way home, I invited her to a dinner party that had been underway for at least an hour and to which I had been invited. To my surprise, she accepted.

"I haven't slept for two days, but what the hell! I'd love a lobster."

We dropped by the house first to leave her stuff and see Sid; and where Lil, true as ever to her nature, spent over an hour in the bathroom changing her dress and "freshening up" for the dinner. We arrived just in time for the last batch of lobsters to come out of the pot; and Lil got to visit with many old friends and neighbors. She had a great time, and on the way home, almost midnight by then, she said, "How come we were never invited to parties like that before in Taunton? Did they exist? Were there always people here in town having fun like that?"

"Yes, I think so. The people on the West Side always had more money for parties like that."

"And obviously a better outlook on life," she said.

We continued this conversation upon returning home where I proudly showed Lil how I had transformed the shed into a lovely new library for my books, records, and booze. After getting her a glass of white wine, and a beer for myself, and putting some instrumental music on the stereo, I mostly listened for the next three hours or so while Cousin Lil told me what she thought about our Maine upbringing.

"Let me tell you," she said, "after a decade of psychiatrists, dumb male doctors, bouts of depression, and attempts at ridding myself of certain well-established hang-ups and habits, I have distinctly mixed feelings about my Downeast roots, as you must have."

"I love it and hate it, about equally," I said.

"I could never live here again. If I ever did, it would be in a town where there is more activity and more anonymity. What I have learned from trying to fit in out west and in Alaska is that we New Englanders, or we Downeasters from Hancock County at least, are so steeped in our rigid background that we can't make it any place, especially socially, and often kill ourselves trying."

"What do you mean exactly?"

"There's nothing physical allowed, always self-control at all times. There's an armor, like chain mail. It's impossible to break out of except through psychoanalysis or an especially good stash of marijuana. With a real high I can feel layers of self-control falling away. Otherwise I'm uptight all the time, even making love. Even sleeping. I wake up with my hands clenched."

She continued: "And then there's the terrible negative world view that people here have. Life is seen as something you have to endure, rather than enjoy. You set yourself up like that and it becomes a self-fulfilling prophecy. You know, it's typified by so many Maine jokes. Even the humor is repressed — or hysterical.

"And then there's the third element. The feeling that we are always inferior, second-rate citizens. We have a 'religion,' if one may call it that, that touts humility at all costs. Don't be proud of your achievements. What makes me want to put my fist through the wall is that I have these talents for which I have been awarded metal cups and pieces of paper, but I'm so inhibited and unsure of myself that I could never do anything about them. The conditioning is so strong that you can't cut through it."

I kept putting the wine to Lil which, instead of lulling her to sleep, seemed to give her more energy to go on.

"That goddamn New England way of dealing with things! Negative, stoic, enduring, accepting. The first way I learned, as you did, from Dad's belt buckle and later from anyone's disapproval, was to keep my mouth shut, to save myself. Hell, I've gone along with people who were essentially crooks or idiots, when my gut feeling was to really tell 'em off. I thought that was the way to be loved."

"Yes, I've done that, too," I said; "and still do it. I hate myself for being used like that, for not standing up to people who do that to me."

"They don't do it to you; you do it to yourself. You let them do it to you."

"Yes, but they sense I won't say anything to them. I'll be nice to them, because I have been taught to be so, and then they'll walk all over me."

"On the other hand," she said, "what I love about Maine is the land. I love the warm, simple, family-centered life that does still exist here, at least on the surface. And the essential goodness of the people. Being raised here has given me a few positive attributes, like honesty, humor, and some sense of ethics in a world that's rapidly losing them."

"But the people are very judgmental."

"Yes, anything out of the norm is to be feared, and therefore, despised. Deep down, I don't think we've progressed all that far from the days of Hester Prynne and her Scarlet Letter. Instead of life being, as I've said, something to enjoy, an unfolding series of adventures, life is a damned struggle, not a pleasure. Of course, we were brought up working class, servants to the summer people, so I've always felt inferior. And the traditional Maine upbringing of a woman, taking all her cues from the men; going along with the men

— put this together with all the sexual repression and inhibition, and look what you've got to face the big, bad world with."

"Of course, many people never leave Maine, or only briefly."

"No. They're afraid to. They don't want to have to compete, to have their world vision altered."

"So who has the best time Downeast?"

"The tourists and some of the summer people who come with their boats and camping equipment to have a good time. They get to use Maine the right way, and get to leave it, too."

"Among the natives, there are certainly all kinds of aberrations and hybrids. Maine homosexuals, for instance, are so closeted and repressed, they turn into heterosexuals."

"Yes, or alcoholics, like everybody else."

"Do you think the repression and poverty causes so much alcoholism in Maine, or do you think it's the awful weather?"

"I think it's a combination. I think the repression causes all kinds of terrible problems, especially in rural Maine: illegitimacy, incest, child abuse, wife beating, suicide . . . just look at our own family. Maine kids are born old. They don't really act like kids. They hold conservative opinions like their parents and talk like old people. Out west, people don't care who your grandfather was. And they do tend to have fewer inhibitions socially and sexually. There are simply more possibilities, more chances to play out one's fantasies, with no one judging you."

"Maine's changing, though, even in our area."

"If that party tonight was any indication, I think you're right; and that, as far as I'm concerned, is all for the good. I would hope that Lovina's kids wouldn't be growing up with all the hang-ups we did. I've made some improvements, I think, but if you notice, I still seem to talk without moving my face or my body. We are so awkward with each other. We can't hug. Look at the way we fumbled to embrace each other at the airport tonight. When mama lay dying in the hospital, she and I couldn't hug. It's not natural to say, 'I love you.' Do you ever remember, Andy, Aunt Sid or Uncle Frank saying that they loved you? Did you hear it from any of our relatives or friends or neighbors?"

"No. You're right. Once I accused Sid of not loving me, and she said, 'We're very proud of your accomplishments.' "

"Sure. They can't say it.

"But then, there's the obsessive need for men. Look at me. The men I meet, the ones I'm attracted to, are attracted to me because they think I'm strong; but when they find out that I'm actually weak and desperate and need them for *their* strength, they want out!

"One time when I was driving up the Alcan Highway with this

fellow in his van, bouncing along on that endless, dangerous dirt road, I got out to go to the bathroom in the woods; but I was feeling so *sensuous* that day that I took off all my clothes and ran around those virgin woods for a bit. There I was somewhere in the north of British Columbia running around naked. Of course, being from New England, I had to make sure, first of all, that I was alone and that no one would see me."

"But you've always run around in the woods."

"Yes, but not nude as an adult. I had to go all the way to British Columbia to dare to do that! Another time, in Hawaii, on Waikiki Beach, I was making love with this fellow in the middle of the night on the beach, when this military sergeant, MP or something, interrupted us with a flashlight in the face. And instead of being outraged at this peeping tom bastard, who told us this was a restricted area, as if they were planning on landing some submarines at any moment, I retreated into that Yankee way of being: extremely fatalistic and controlled, standing there with the blanket clutched about me, answering his foolish questions in clipped, crisp tones, as I had been brought up to do."

"Do you think Maine people would be as good and self-effacing as they are if they weren't so repressed? If they didn't have such an inferiority complex?"

"I don't know. Maine people work hard and do a good job, because they're afraid not to. It's drummed into us. Get to work early, do more than your share, don't have to be told after the first time, don't expect a raise. Give; don't take; don't expect any handouts. Struggle and die. People in small towns, of course, need each other, even if they don't like each other. You keep your mouth shut, because you might need their help some day. Of course, you do talk behind their backs, which is the one thing I think I dislike most here. But in a small town, everyone knows you, and your relatives. You'd get a reputation if you weren't a good worker, or lazy, or not honest. Everyone remembers what you did or didn't do at school."

"Maine people out-of-state, many of them anyway, totally reject Maine, try to change their accents and so on.

"And yet, the people who have moved here and adopted Maine feel awful that they're not natives. They think it's some kind of weird honor to be born here."

"Yes, Maine has a hold on one, and because of the hold it has on me, I'm always living in two places. I'm there physically, but emotionally I'm often still here. I don't fit in there, but I can't live here any more either."

"I had the same problem when I was living in upstate New York, even though it wasn't out west. People were always introducing me as 'Andy from Maine,' like I was inseparable from my birthplace, or as if it were a special calling."

"I know. People come up to me in Alaska and ask right away if I'm from New England. They can evidently smell it or know from the firm set of my jaw."

"Well, you are home again."

"Yep, so I am. Home again. The Maine native returned. Good God, I'll never get this nasty, beautiful place out of my system! I must somehow come to terms with it, my shrinks say, so here I am, back home in herring choker land . . ."

At about this time, Sid appeared in the doorway in her housecoat and slippers, her head done up in some kind of nightcap that made her look as old as God's wet nurse. Lillie and I were in the salt water again, and Sid was about to procure another alder switch.

"Don't you two realize what time it is? It's almost three o'clock in the morning! Don't you think it's time you both went to bed! I can't sleep with this light on in here! And I've got to get up early!"

All Lil and I could do was look at each other and smile, deeply.

STEP-OVER TOE-HOLD

EVEN IN MID-NOVEMBER when it was getting cold, I'd climb up the unpainted, broken-down shed stairs after supper with a flashlight to the shed chamber where I'd play for hours with my homemade television studio, so strong was the pull of my fantasy world. There I'd plan variety, dramatic, and panel shows directed by me; design miniature sets for my cardboard actors attired in their aluminum foil and crepe paper costumes. Using mostly cardboard, scotch tape, toothpicks, foil, wax paper, multi-colored index cards, cookie package dividers, bits of cloth and glass, I devised an elaborate multi-floored dollhouse. I even wrote scripts for the shows and made dressing rooms for my stars.

One night, as I was making my way across the shed, amidst cries from my mother from the adjoining pantry that it was too cold to play up there, I hesitated briefly before my father who was busy skinning out a deer he had just killed early in the hunting season. He had most of the fur coat skinned off and was cutting the meat and putting pieces of it in a big enamel pan on the floor beside him. Newspapers covered the floor. My father, as usual, had on his old baseball cap and a cigarette hanging out of his mouth. The deer, which was a pretty fair-sized buck, was hanging from a bolt on one of the middle beams across the shed ceiling. I had once tried to help my father skin out a deer, but it had made me sick to my stomach, and so he didn't ask me anymore. "Where ya going?" he asked. "Up to the shed chamber to play with dolls?"

I didn't answer him. I just went upstairs. Through the cracks in the floor I could see him hacking away at the deer; and because he was short of breath and always smoking, he'd cough and grunt. He had already suffered one mild heart attack and my mother was always worried about him. Finally, he'd hollar up at me, "O.K., I'm going in now and I'm turning the light off. You come down now."

He'd give my mother the fresh meat to wrap up in aluminum foil and label and put in the freezer compartment of our old Gibson refrigerator while he and I would go into the living room and watch television. A great outdoorsman who loved fishing and hunting, my father never liked team sports; and even when my older brother and I were on teams in school, he'd never go to see us play. But he did like watching boxing and wrestling matches on television. In the mid-Fifties, there were boxing matches on Wednesday and Friday nights and wrestling bouts on all the time. Two men beating each other around a ring made sense to my father. The Wednesday night matches were sponsored by Pabst Blue Ribbon and the Friday night fights were sponsored by Gillette. I'd go off to bed with their jingle of "Look sharp! Feel sharp! Be sharp!" ringing in my head. After one fighter was declared the winner, my father would always say, in his dry, dead-pan voice, "What a man!"

The wrestling matches I enjoyed more than the boxing exhibitions, because I enjoyed all the show biz and dress-up that went with them. Gorgeous George was like Liberace as a wrestler and Ricki Starr wrestled in pink tights and ballet slippers. There were also crazy midgets and tough women wrestlers in spangled bathing suits. The melodrama, week after week, was, of course, unending. There was always a grudge match that would continue for weeks; the villains were ever-so dastardly and the heroes so clean-cut and full of fair play. My favorite at the time was the handsome blonde muscleman named Edouard Carpentier from Montreal who was billed as "The Flying Frenchman," because of the way he could execute back flips, drop kicks, and cartwheels mixed in with the more conventional takedowns, headlocks, and bearhugs. It was always very exciting when the "body beautiful" Frenchman tangled with the villainous Killer Kowalski, who would commit all manner of illegal atrocities against the handsome hero to the great boos and screams of the crowd. Kowalski's most punishing hold was the dreaded "claw hold," which, when applied to the other wrestler's stomach, was the end of the line for Kowalski's foe.

There were other wrestling terms, too, which were a part of the amusement: terms like "flying double arm wringer," "double hiproll," "flying head scissors," and every wrestler's specialty hold. It might be Kowalski's "claw hold" or someone else's "cobra clutch" or "congo butt" or "Italian pile driver." All of the wrestlers that we liked to watch in the '50's seemed to enjoy using airplane spins, flying dropkicks, and body scissors. And someone was always using the step-over toe-hold, a very ineffectual-looking hold, but one which was supposed to give some authority and power over an opponent. At least it held an opponent at bay until the wrestlers could think of what else to do before it was time for one or the other to win the pin.

My father also loved watching William Bendix of "The Life of Riley" and Jackie Gleason and Art Carney in the "Honeymooners" skits. He'd sit there in his rocking chair in his pajamas, sipping on his Narragansett, and laughing his head off as Gleason ranted and raved at his long-suffering wife played by Audrey Meadows. My mother hated Jackie Gleason.

When I was old enough, my father took me out in the backfield and showed me how to shoot with a rifle. When I was very little, he let me use a .22 and I would shoot at tin cans and bottles lined up on the neighbor's fence. One time I got to try his beloved .300 Savage, which literally knocked me on my rear end. The few times, however, that I went hunting with him, while I loved being in the November woods, I was scared to death, especially when the men would start drinking and then driving for a deer, racing and yelling through the woods with their loaded rifles. My father would shoot at anything. One time walking down a woods road he spotted a chipmunk and shot it. I was horrified and ran over to the bloody body. With his dying breath, the chipmunk bit me. "For Christ's sake, that'll teach ya!" my father said. "Now you'll probably get rabies or something." That same walk he shot at a loon out on the lake. The other male relatives and neighbors really respected my father's prowess with a hunting rifle. He always got his deer, and usually more than one. So, once in the woods, with an audience, it was like he had to show off. He really lived all of his life for November.

One of the last times I went hunting with him and his boss and other men friends I really embarrassed him. I got scared and hid under a log when there was a drive on; and he found me there crouching. He was disgusted, even though he never said anything.

In the hunting camp where my father would hole up for a week or two, he always seemed to play the role of cook, or "cookee," as he called it. "Cookee" was a term used on the old Maine Central steam boats that my father used to work on as a young man.

And there was fishing. My father had once caught one of the biggest bass ever recorded from East Grand Lake Stream. We had pictures of the beast all over the house and my father and uncles were always looking at the pictures and discussing the magnitude of the catch. Once, as a little fisher myself with a bamboo fishing rod, I wanted to impress the old man, so while he had gone off with his boss for an all-day fishing trip one summer day, I sat on the dock at the camp and caught about a dozen suckers, which I thought were pretty impressive-looking fish. I put them in a pail which I hid out back of the woodshed to show him when he got back. But, alas, by the time he returned, a couple of cats had discovered my cache and removed all of the suckers. Again, I had only an empty vessel to show him.

So I started taking piano lessons.

I was thirteen or so and I loved music. We had an old, untuned, upright piano with a couple of missing keys, and I wanted to know how to play it. So I talked my mother into letting me use some of my summer lawn-mowing money for the one dollar a week after school lesson. My father hated the idea and he hated my practicing. The schoolbus from Taunton Corner would drop me off at Taunton Junction, where my father worked for the Rudolph Keen Fuel Oil Company, and I would walk the mile or so down the hill, across the Taunton Bridge, to West Hamlin and the big green house where Mrs. Scott, who reminded me of Loretta Young in both looks and mannerisms, would give me my lesson. Afterwards, I walked back across the bridge to the Fuel Oil Company, hung around while my father "cashed up" with Virginia, the long-time, old maid secretary and treasurer of the firm. Sometimes Virginia would give me little gifts if I had to wait for my father who was having an unexpected or late delivery. She once gave me a Planter's Peanut Coloring Book with Mr. Peanut cavorting about New York; and often she gave me money for a candy bar or a free Coke from the machine. When it was time for my father to go home, he let me sit up front with him with my red John Thompson music books while three of his greasy colleagues (everyone was greasy around the garage and trucks, of course) with their dinner pails would crowd into the back seat. There would always be a few humorous remarks about my music lessons, usually from my father. There I was embarrassing him again.

In the seventh grade, I announced one night at the supper table that I was going to become a writer. My father just looked across at me, his hair hanging in his face as usual, and said, "You'd better be a schoolteacher or minister." That was a major insult since he was always saying how stupid teachers were and how ministers were either crooks or queers. In the eighth grade I announced I was going to college. My father greeted this by saying, "Ya better get that notion out of ya head. Only rich kids go to college. Unless ya haven't noticed it, we ain't rich."

All of my younger life, and even up through high school, I had very few new clothes to call my own. I always wore hand-me-downs from my brother, family friends, or the summer people. But in the ninth grade I did buy myself with my own money my first pair of new Levis, and upon seeing me in them, my father said, "Those pants are too tight about the crotch! Take 'em off!" Also, up until high school, my father gave me all of my haircuts on Sundays in our "kitchen barbershop." And he made sure he gave me a haircut, all right. When he finished with me, I looked like a skinned monkey. When I'd complain, he'd say, "Well, ya wanted a haircut, didn't ya?"

When I made the JV basketball team in high school, my father tried to talk me into quitting by telling me repeatedly that I'd "break something and be maimed for life." I think he just didn't want to have to come pick me up after practices. As a member of the cross country team, I'd often try to practice running, as I was supposed to, on the weekends; but my father made me stop. "Running down the road that way," he said, "the neighbors will think our house is on fire!"

One night I was holding the flashlight for him while he tried to fix the engine of our old 1951 Mercury. At one point, I moved the light a bit, and he yelled at me. "You think I'm stupid, don't ya?" I yelled back. "Yes, I think you're goddamn stupid if ya can't even hold a flashlight steady for five minutes," he said. I threw the flashlight down and ran into the house. Another time I swore at him at the kitchen table, and in an instant found myself on my back on the kitchen floor with my father on top of me, a cigarette dangling out of his mouth, and the ashes falling on my face. I was sixteen by then and around six feet, so I was shocked by my father's ability to take me down so fast and pin me so solidly. And I was surprised to realize how strong he was, how I couldn't move a muscle under him. "You're lucky I didn't give ya a goddamn super piledriver!" he said.

I'd watch him eat in the morning. He always made this oatmeal concoction with brown sugar, melted butter, the whole thing swimming in canned milk. At supper he loved to sop up the gravy with pieces of bread. He loved anything soggy, sweet, and fattening.

I helped him paint and shingle our house. I helped him with all the seasonal chores: banking the house with tarpaper and brush in the fall, taking the banking off in the spring, burning the backfield as soon as the snow was gone. I washed and waxed the car. As I got older, I gradually did all of the mowing, clipping and raking; and I helped both of my parents with their caretaking chores at two summer places on Taunton Point.

Once I accompanied him on one of his night fuel oil deliveries in the middle of the winter downeast to Cherryfield or Harrington or some place; and it seemed like we drove forever. Dad did sing a few of his tunes. He'd always sing the two lines or so that he knew over and over. One of them was, "I'm a poor little girl waiting for bread." He'd smoke his Camel cigarettes and keep asking me if I were too cold or too warm. He also drove that Texaco truck right in the middle of the road and at about twenty miles over the speed limit. He never drove all that fast when with Mom because she'd scream at him not to go over forty.

She'd also scream at him to cut his meat up into smaller pieces at supper and she'd scream at him when he'd come home every year drunk from his Texaco banquets.

I was thrilled to read after school one day a headline story on the front page of the Bangor *Daily News* about my father. Dad was a hero! COURAGEOUS TRUCK DRIVER STOPS BLAZE the headline read and the story went on to relate how my father had stopped a potentially explosive gasoline fire which had started at the Texaco fuel oil storage area in Bangor. When he came home that night, I congratulated him by saying, "Dad! You're a hero!" "Yeah," he said, "but you notice they forget to tell ya who started the fire." Then I noticed the ever-present cigarette dangling from his lips. "It's a wonder I didn't blow myself up," he said.

Spending a weekend home from college during my freshman year, I was sitting across the living room from my father watching him reading a Rommel book with his W. T. Grant three dollar eyeglasses on when he looked at me and said, "Yes, I know. I'm a complete failure."

But he actually never failed to help me when I really needed help.

When the battery on my first car, a 1959 Ford Galaxie, which I bought the last semester of my senior year at the University of Maine, went flat the night before I was to start my student teaching in Bangor, he drove all the way to Orono after work to install a new battery in my car and make sure everything was going to go o.k. in the morning.

By the time I was in my mid-twenties, and Dad was nearing sixty, I realized that I didn't have much more time in which to try and become friends with him. I knew we would never be close pals, that he'd never hug me or say he loved me; but I did want him to look upon me at least once with some faint glimmer of approval.

From one of my first paychecks I sent him a ten dollar check for his birthday and it bounced. I sent him books: General MacArthur's *Reminiscences*, Truman Capote's *In Cold Blood*, and other books

I thought he'd enjoy and that we could talk about. Whenever I was home for occasional vacations, I'd try to get him to talk about his life working on the steamboats, working on the old lumber wharves over to Ellsworth, driving his trucks all over Maine.

One summer when I was home from my teaching job in New York, I got him to go with me for a beer and a boxing match in Ellsworth. The beer was good, and he seemed to be enjoying himself; but the boxing matches disgusted us both. The Job Corps then had an outlet in Bar Harbor and an Ellsworth boxing promoter, who also ran the movie theater, sold foundation garments, and served as the Boy Scout leader, arranged to have the Black and Puerto Rican Job Corps boys fight some Maine Indian boys in the old Grand Theatre before a predominantly white redneck audience. The promoter kept taking up a collection for the Jimmy Fund, and the boys pounded each other around the ring while the worst kind of racist comments were hurled back and forth. My father and I left early.

When he turned sixty-one, and had been holding down a regular job since he was thirteen, I asked my father about his plans. "I'm going to retire next year," he said, "and then drop dead the year after."

He sure knew how to call 'em.

We were sitting together two years later on the couch at my brother's place outside of Cape Kennedy in Florida right after Christmas 1969 when Dad suddenly said, when he and Mom were talking about visiting along the way back to Maine, "I'd like to drive up to Syracuse and see An-day's apartment and have a few beers with him."

Ah, the line I had been longing to hear all of my grown up life. My father actually wanting to do something with me in my world. I was thrilled.

But he never made it. That Christmas vacation was the last time I saw him alive. Shaking his hand just before I got into my brother's car to drive to the Orlando Airport to return to Syracuse, I sensed this was it. And so I stared back at him, standing there next to a palm tree, his hair in his face, the cigarette dangling from his lips, his hands in his pockets, his stomach hanging over his belt, unsmiling forever, as my mother beside him waved and waved goodbye.

He died of a heart attack a few days later, in a South Carolina motel on the way back to Downeast. My mother told me that he had cried uncontrollably the night before and that it had frightened her. The night that my brother called to tell me of our father's death, I did the same.

BOOKS BY PUCKERBRUSH PRESS

THE THOUSAND SPRINGS	short stories	Mary Gray Hughes
THE INVADERS	short storeis	Marjorie Kaplan
DRIFTWOOD	Maine stories	Edward Holmes
CIMMERIAN	poems	Constance Hunting
AN OLD PUB NEAR THE ANGEL	short stories	James Kelman
DORANDO: A SPANISH TALE	novel	James Boswell edited by Robert Hunting
THE CROSSING	poems	Albert Stainton Rita Stainton
THE MOUNTAIN, THE STONE	short stories	Kathleen Kranidas
A DAY'S WORK	poems	Michael McMahon
A PAPER RAINCOAT	poems	Sonya Dorman
BEYOND THE SUMMERHOUSE	poem	Constance Hunting
A STRANGER HERE, MYSELF	short stories	Thelma Nason
farmwife	poem	lee sharkey
GREENGROUND-TOWN	short stories	Christopher Fahy
BETWEEN SUNDAYS	short narratives	Douglas Young
ONE TO THE MANY	poems	Anne Hazlewood-Brady
NOTES FROM SICK ROOMS	essay	Mrs. Leslie Stephen
TWO PLAYS	plays	Arnold Colbath
WRITINGS ON WRITING	essays	May Sarton
box of roses	poems	lee sharkey
DEAD OF WINTER	poems	Michael McMahon
DARKWOOD	poems	Michael Alpert
THE POLICE KNOW EVERYTHING	Downeast stories	Sanford Phippen
THE ROCKING HORSE	sermons for children	Douglas Young
IN A DARK TIME	anthology	Virgil Bisset and Constance Hunting, editors
LIGHT YEARS	poems	Roberta Chester
MY LIFE AS A MAINE-IAC	autobiography/history	Muriel Young
PALACE OF EARTH	poems	Sonya Dorman
DEAREST ANDREW	letters	V. Sackville-West edited by Nancy MacKnight
THE DEATH OF MICHELANGELO	sonnet sequence	Jonathan Aldrich
A PRIMER OF CHRISTIANITY AND ETHICS	essays	Douglas Young
LETTERS TO MAY	letters	Eleanor Mabel Sarton
TURNIP PIE	short stories	Rebecca Cummings

SANFORD PHIPPEN was raised in Hancock, Maine where he still summers and where he works as Hancock Point librarian. He is the first President of The Historical Society of the Town of Hancock and was one of the principal researchers and writers for the 1978 Sesquicentennial book, *A History of the Town of Hancock.* A graduate of Sumner Memorial High School in East Sullivan, Maine, and of the University of Maine at Orono, he received his M.A. in English Education from Syracuse University.

It might be said that his professional writing career began at the end of his seventh grade year at Hancock Grammar School in 1955 when he won the Second Prize of $3.00 for a book report on Abraham Lincoln. The same year, a drawing of his (an untraveled, rural Maine boy's concept of life in Miami Beach) was published "On the Easel" in the then Portland *Sunday Telegram.* In high school he served as co-editor in his senior year of the high school yearbook, *The Spindrift*; and in college, he wrote for the *Maine Campus* newspaper. His regular column of the ROTC Army news was called "Bugle Blasts of the Brass."

For fifteen years, Phippen taught high school English in central New York, first in the New Hartford system, where he also coached cross country and advised the literary magazine, *SCOP*; and then in the city of Syracuse, where he founded and advised the literary magazine, *Reflections*, and advised the school newspaper, *The Quill.* He now teaches English at Orono High School where he advises the school newspaper, *Inside*, and co-advises the literary magazine, *Enclave.* Both Orono publications were founded by Phippen.

Long involved during his teaching career as a director, actor, and co-director of many shows and plays, for the 1978 Hancock Sesquicentennial, he wrote and directed a review, "Agreen and Us." He has been book editor of *Maine Life* magazine since 1976. Other articles, reviews, and stories of his have appeared in the New York *Times, Puckerbrush Review, Fence Industry* magazine, Ellsworth *American, Maine Alumnus, Tuesday Weekly,* and the Bangor *Daily News.* In 1980, an article of Phippen's, "Missing From the Books: My Maine," appeared first in *Puckerbrush Review* and later in *Maine Life*, and in 1981 became the basis of a six-part radic series with Virgil Bisset on MPBN-FM radio entitled "The Maine That's Missing."

Text set on Compuwriter in 10 point English, titles in Stymie Medium
Photocomposition and page makeup by Merle Hillman